Howling FOR MORE

A LILY QUINN NOVEL

NATALIE & ERIC SEVERINE

LOOSE LEAF
STORIES

Chapter ONE

Myrrh and cinquefoil to capture my target. A circle of salt to isolate and wormwood to banish, with runes in pearlash and blue vitriol to guide the way.

The sweet smell of herbs wasn't enough to overpower the thick, wet musk of the bayou. Moss and lichen and tangled leaves floated on the murky water. I inscribed interlocking raido and ehwaz runes across the deck of the rental boat, my ebony charcoal scratching the wood's already peeling finish.

So much for my security deposit... but the boat's deck was the only place to draw out my spell in the damp green of the Louisiana bayou. I had dragged it up onto the muddy shore, scraping the hull on submerged tree roots and soaking my pants to the knee. But I could buy a new boat and a whole wardrobe of designer clothes with the reward money that the College was offering for this werewolf's capture.

Most bounty hunters work for gold, but I would have caught werewolves for free. My name is Stefano Rossi and I will spend my life hunting them. I'll probably die chasing lycanthropes and it will be a life well spent. There is no monster on earth more destructive than werewolves and no one that knows it better than I do.

The uneven ground and shifting waterways of the swamp were making this a complicated hunt. After four days in the bayou, my clothes and hair were permanently soaked with sweat and water. I hoped the humidity and cacophony of earthy scents wouldn't throw my target off my trail, but the terrain and weather slowed me down, making me that much easier to track. The werewolf had to be close by now.

I slashed lines of seared ebony across the runed circle, binding them together. The demon wolf had my scent and last night's divination showed it here at noon. At least, I hoped this was the spot. There was a huge cottonwood tree on the other side of the slow-moving brown water that looked familiar from my magical vision, but I couldn't be sure. Still, the wolf had been tracking me for an hour or more. Doubtlessly preparing to pounce even now.

Good.

I was the bait in my own trap, hunting the wolf as it hunted me. Being both hunter and prey made an already perilous task suicidally dangerous, but I've been doing this for fifteen years and I'm the best bounty hunter in the College. Well, I might have *some* competition for the number one slot, but she's not a wizard.

The orange afternoon sun turned the still air hot and heavy, but overlapping cypress branches cast deep, crisscrossing shadows that rippled across the murky water. Ripples...? Something was moving out there in the swamp. A brackish wave slapped against the side of my beached boat, rocking the deck beneath me. Whatever moved through the water was big – too big to be an alligator. Not that the local wildlife had made me feel particularly welcome, as the bite marks in the boat and the leather of my boots could attest.

I balanced on the balls of my feet and inscribed the final runes of my spell circle, then straightened to inspect my work. It was a potentially costly second of preoccupation when there was a werewolf nearby, but a single error in my magic could be equally disastrous. All four interlocking rings of angled runes – written out in ebony charcoal scorched under the new moon – were dark and neat. My spell was ready. I had nine minutes to finish and execute the teleportation before the myrrh lost its potency and I would have to start all over again.

A heron burst from the tangled Spanish moss with a soft thunderclap and a white blur of motion. And then another wild shape bounded through the swamp on four long, powerful limbs. Upright, I guessed that the werewolf was eight and a half feet tall – a little on the small side for a lycanthrope, but no less deadly. The wolf's fur was slicked against its muscular body with water and yellow-gold eyes gleamed like lanterns in the shadowed afternoon.

The werewolf leapt over a fallen cypress tree, kicking up huge sprays of water and mud as it raced toward my boat. I stood my ground in the center of the runic circles and drew the revolver from under my arm. The forty-five caliber bullets were pure, alchemically tempered sterling silver. Nothing else could slow a werewolf down.

Only silver could kill a lycanthrope, and even then only if I put enough of it straight into the beast's brain or heart. But I didn't fly all the way out to Louisiana and boat for days through the bayou, fending off mosquitoes and alligators equally intent on eating me alive, just to kill this werewolf.

Like all werewolves, this was an ordinary human, transformed by a cruel demonic curse into a savage killing machine. I was here to save them.

The werewolf charged at me through muddy water and weeds. It tore a low-hanging branch out of its path with one paw the size of a dinner plate and tipped in two-inch-long claws. Those molten gold eyes were fixed on me with a hatred burning like hellfire and the werewolf let out a growl so deep that it shook my bones.

Something splashed behind me, up on the shore, but I didn't dare take my eyes off the werewolf closing in at roughly freeway speeds. Another alligator, maybe? No, the sound was coming closer.

Most animals ran, flew or swam as fast as they could away from a werewolf. Even alligators – being the apex predator means jack shit when a werewolf enters your ecosystem.

No time to worry about that now. The werewolf was moving too quickly, even through the weed-choked swamp, and hurling up an impressive fan of brackish water. It would bury its claws to the wrist in my guts before I could complete my incantation.

I squared my shoulders, sighted down the revolver and pulled the trigger. The barrel kicked skyward and the shot rang in my ears. My prey didn't recoil at all from the impact – it takes a lot to stagger a six-hundred-pound werewolf – but its loping gait faltered. The third of an ounce of silver in my shot would slow it down for sixty-seven seconds. Approximately.

The werewolf slammed hard into the side of my boat, sending it sliding several yards back through the mud and moss. I rocked on my feet, but managed to stay upright. There was more splashing, now coming from beside my boat, but then the werewolf's hooked claws sank into the deck railing, throwing splinters into the air.

Time to finish this. It would be close, but it always was. I raised my empty hand and began to chant.

"Stefano!"

I almost stopped chanting. What the hell...? Werewolves can't talk. I've only heard a demon wolf speak once and only then because he was possessed by a ghost... Long story.

Besides, I knew that voice. I wasn't stupid enough to take my eyes off the werewolf vaulting up over the boat's railing – that was just as dangerous as halting my spell halfway done – but I turned to catch a glimpse of the movement in my peripheral vision: a mud-covered man wading through the waist-deep water as fast as his long legs would carry him.

Dominic.

The twenty-something bottle-blond clutched a shotgun against his chest to keep it dry. Dominic wasn't a wizard or a bounty hunter, but he had been cursed with lycanthropy. Twice. The second time, the idiot boy had actually volunteered for it in order to help a mutual friend. The College of Merlinic wizards had lifted his curse both times... So what the hell was he doing out here?

I didn't dare interrupt my incantation long enough to answer Dominic, so I waved him urgently away with one hand as the werewolf slammed down onto the deck. The rental boat was beached and mired in about a foot of mud, but the whole thing rocked hard under the impact. Dominic slewed to a stop in the water and raised his shotgun.

"Stefano, look out!" he shouted.

Dominic aimed and fired. Buckshot ripped through the werewolf and flung bright red blood up into the air, but unless that shell was packed with silver, he was only pissing it off.

And that was exactly what happened.

The beast skidded to a sudden halt and spun toward Dominic. Rage burned in the werewolf's yellow eyes and it reared up to let out a long, terrible howl. Then the lycanthrope dropped back to four paws and leapt at its new prey.

Dominic swore, but he stood his ground, pumped his shotgun and then fired again. The werewolf snarled and more blood spattered the bayou, but the beast didn't slow down. My silver shot was swiftly wearing off. There was no stopping my incantation now... but if I didn't lure that werewolf back into range, I would succeed only in teleporting a few mosquitoes to the waiting magical prison while a monster busily tore Dominic into bite-sized pieces.

I dropped my revolver and drew a knife from my belt. The blade was coated in silver, too, but that didn't matter right now. Dominic fired off a third shot, but then he had to throw himself down into the mud as the werewolf closed and slashed out with its long meat-hook claws. Dominic rolled onto his back in the muck and raised his shotgun again. All signs of his previous hits had vanished from the werewolf's wet pelt, healed away within seconds.

I sliced the knife blade along the outside of my forearm. It hurt, but I couldn't spare the time or breath to swear. I was already slowing the spell incantation as much as I dared. Blood ran down my arm and spattered at my feet inside the charcoal circles.

Snarling, the werewolf whirled toward me again, drawn inexorably by the scent of fresh blood. It bared sharp teeth and growled out a low, hungry sound. I raised my cut arm and tightened my fingers into a fist. Red streamed down my skin and soaked my sleeve.

The werewolf leapt away from Dominic and charged at me. Between one heartbeat and the next, the mud-slicked monster was across the waterway and leaping onto the boat once more. Its lantern eyes burned with savage hunger and violence. The werewolf flexed its claws, ripping deep gouges into the boat's deck, and then lunged at me.

With a final shout, I finished the incantation. Drops of blood and water floated up into the air like beads on invisible strings, and my gun rose gently from the ground. Even the werewolf's deadly pounce slowed and then stopped. The beast howled in fury, but there was a flash of colorless light and then the werewolf vanished.

Swamp water and gun and rotting cypress leaves splashed down around me. The charcoal and herbs were all gone, consumed by my spell, but the rental boat was still trashed. Well worth it to get the job done, but...

I jumped down to shore as Dominic managed to right himself and come sloshing back to more or less solid ground. I grabbed the boy by one shoulder and gave him a hard shake. Mud and water flew from Dominic's hair.

"Dude, that was badass!" he announced with a wide grin.

"What the hell do you think you're doing?" I snarled.

"Helping," Dominic said. "I'm your new partner!"

Chapter
TWO

The College used to be further out from the city before modern civilization began its inexorable creep across the wilderness. Now, it's not even much of a drive.

The College is a huge old estate filled with so many libraries, studies and even our own observatory that you might mistake it for an actual college. Which it was, I supposed. But what I had learned here wasn't taught in any other school on the continent.

I stalked down the corridor of Dresden Hall, past the long line of polished suits of antique armor, all wearing their red and white surcoats. Along the opposite wall ran the College's bounty board, an ancient and massive corkboard, thick with hand-written parchment notices for the capture of dangerous monsters, rogue fairies and evil spirits.

Dominic jogged to keep up with me. "You *need* a sidekick, man."

The blond surfer had followed me all the way out of Louisiana and now back to the College, furiously intent on... helping.

"I'm the Robin to your Batman, dude," Dominic told me. Again. "Or maybe Wolfman, since you mostly hunt werewolves. Wait, Batman doesn't fight bats... Anyway, that's not the point!"

"I don't need a partner." I was repeating myself, too.

"These bounties are dangerous. Some of them just aren't one-wizard jobs, Stefano! You and Lily had to team up to catch me the first time I was cursed, remember?"

I remembered and let out a short grunt to acknowledge that small bit of truth. Dominic grinned.

"Exactly," he announced. "You need a partner!"

"No. If you want a share of the werewolf's bounty, I can arrange it – if that will get you to leave me alone. Don't expect a large percentage, though. All you did was get in my way."

Dominic looked crestfallen at that and lagged behind a few paces, but quickly shook it off and ran to catch up once more. His expression was determined again.

"I don't want the gold," Dominic said.

That was a little surprising. Alchemy could transform most base metals into gold. While the Merlinic order carefully regulated how much they created to avoid glutting the market, the College was still very, very rich. It was hard to believe that a non-wizard like Dominic was turning down that kind of money.

"Then what is this about?" I asked.

"Look, I already work for the College," Dominic said. "But it's just measuring and carrying stuff for people who are way too important to be doing that shit."

I nodded. Remember when I said that lycanthropy was a curse? Well, even after Dominic's first transformation – to say nothing of volunteering for round two – there was far too much residual demonic energies in his body for our mind-altering spells to work. It was unlikely that Dominic felt anything out of the ordinary, but his immutable memories meant that he knew things few other humans do, and that the College had to keep an eye on him. Might as well give the kid a job.

"What? Don't they pay you enough?" I asked.

"No, the money is fine," said Dominic. "It's the job that's not enough. I mean, it was for a while. Working here, for the wizards...

It's the first thing I've ever done that felt like it was *worth* something. Like, actually important. I want to help."

I scratched my beard and scowled. Dominic had that dumb, earnest puppy-dog look on his face again. He meant every word. Dominic wouldn't go back to filing books and measuring out saltpeter any more than he would return to surfing and serving coffee. He was determined to become a hunter and protect the world from monsters.

"Help somebody else," I said.

"But–!" Dominic protested.

"I work alone."

"That's bullshit! You worked with Lily! And what about all that stuff that went down with Asmodai last year?"

I stopped and whirled to face Dominic. He slid to a halt on the smooth-polished floor only barely in time to avoid crashing into me. Dominic stared with wide eyes.

"You were killing College wizards," I said. "You were a menace to the entire city and left me no choice but to accept Lilith's help in hunting you down."

Dominic recoiled like I had just punched him and I almost felt bad for what I had said. But this was important. I kept my voice and my expression hard.

"Asmodai threatened all of existence," I said. "Yes, under those kinds of truly exceptional circumstances, I will work with other hunters. But it's always dangerous and difficult. Merlinic magic requires absolute care and precision. Imagine if someone else's nightshade got mixed into my cinquefoil."

"But I'm not a wizard!" Dominic told me. "I'm not going to get my magic stuff mixed up with yours. I can't even cast spells! I don't have the head for magic."

Shocking.

"I can help you!" Dominic insisted. "I'll do the scutwork for all of your spells. I've measured shit-tons of cinquefoil and nightshade.

I can tell them apart in my sleep, man. And I can shoot a gun. I even brought silver slugs down to Louisiana. Over a gram of silver in each one! I'm not stupid!"

My blood went cold. I grabbed Dominic's arm and yanked him in close.

"Yes, you are," I hissed. "If you managed to put that much silver into a werewolf's head or heart, you could have killed it!"

"It was going to kill *you*, Stefano!"

"I don't kill werewolves."

Not anymore. But I had once, when I was sixteen and frightened and didn't know any better. I wasn't a wizard back then, just a scared kid on a hunting trip with my parents that went horribly wrong. When my mother's demonic werewolf rage ran its course and she finally passed out, I slit her throat with my knife. Only later did I discover that the College could have lifted the curse and saved her. But by then, it was far too late.

Never again.

The hallway ended in two smaller branches, flanking a pair of wide oak doors with an iron knocker forged elaborately into the shape of a gargoyle. Its dark metal eyes swiveled from me to Dominic and narrowed. I knocked on the door, though about a dozen spells would already have warned the occupants of my approach. But it was respectful.

"You'll get some of the bounty," I told Dominic. "That's the last I want to hear about any of this."

He shook his head. "Keep your gold, dude."

Dominic turned and walked back the way we had come. I have to admit that it didn't feel great, but I was doing us both a favor. Hunting monsters was dangerous work, and catching werewolves even worse. Dominic was better off at the College. Here, he was safe and wouldn't get in my way.

Satisfied that I was alone now, the big oak doors swung open to allow me entry into the council chamber. It was a large room hung all along its paneled walls with the portraits of every High Magus, going all the way back to the formation of the College by our predecessors, the Castle.

In the center of the room stood the massive circular table, a monolithic reminder of the Round Table of Camelot that came even before the Castle. Most of the seats were empty, but a tall woman stood beside the table like she was waiting for me. My breath caught at the sight of her. Still, after all this time.

Sylvia North would have been my first vote to succeed Vincent Myrdon as High Magus when he stepped down, if there had been a vote. Sylvia was brilliant, commanding and ravishing. Alright, that last part wasn't exactly important for a leader, but I couldn't help noticing. I *always* noticed Sylvia's dark eyes and skin, curling black hair with the striking lock of silver at her brow. The look she gave me over her glasses was cool and purely professional, but still made my pants feel suddenly far too tight.

Sylvia used to be a bounty hunter. Seventeen years ago, she was on the prowl for a werewolf in the mountains east of the city. Sylvia tracked down and captured her prey, but she also discovered a teenage boy shivering and crying over his mother's body, a bloody knife still clutched in his hand.

She could have just taken my memory of that day. In many ways, that would have been kinder. But instead, Sylvia brought me back to the College and promised that if I worked hard enough, I could fight the werewolf curse. Unlike Dominic, I had the talent for magic. I started as an assistant, too, but Sylvia taught me to be a wizard. And a hunter.

Sylvia North made me the man I am today, but I still felt sixteen years old every time I saw her: awed, inspired and terribly aroused. I wonder if I'll ever be able to face her without blushing.

"Stefano," Sylvia said. "Another successful hunt. Your quarry has arrived safely in the Tower and the ritual for his cure will begin on the new moon."

"It was a close thing," I admitted. "Closer than usual."

Sylvia nodded once and swept her hand over a stack of shining gold bars on the rune-carved table. "Your reward, one and a quarter million dollars at today's value."

Monster hunting was dangerous, but it paid well. Werewolves were particularly deadly and lucrative, second only to ancient vampires. Even after the cost of rare herbs, chemicals and replacing the ruined motorboat, I still had more than enough to buy a new truck. I had to get one every year – not out of any particular sense of style or masculine pride, but because that's about how long they lasted before being torn apart by monsters.

The rest of my money – which was more than I knew what to do with, really – sat in several banks, each managed by College-initiated accountants. I hadn't checked the balance in a few months, but it was more than enough to retire in luxury if I ever wanted to.

I tapped a fingernail against a slim golden bar and listened to the soft metallic ring. I only had one retirement plan and it didn't call for a lot of money. Not more than the cost of my burial, at least.

"There's something else Sylvia and I need to discuss with you."

I almost jumped at the second voice. Dorian Vandi, the new High Magus of the College, sat in a large chair opposite the door. I wasn't sure if Dorian had just arrived or if I had simply overlooked the naturally quiet old wizard. Probably the latter and probably while I was busy blushing at Sylvia.

I bowed my head respectfully to the High Magus. When Dorian had taken leadership of the College, Sylvia assumed his job managing and paying the bounty hunters. So what could Dorian have to say to me?

"What is it?" I asked.

Sylvia seated herself and Dorian gestured for me to do the same. I obeyed at once. The new High Magus smiled through the slightly unkempt white of his beard and rubbed the heel of his hand over his balding pate. Dorian was short and awkward and a profoundly powerful wizard. At a glance, it was hard to tell that Dorian Vandi had been a hunter like me in his youth, feared by undead and Unseelie from coast to coast. But only if you didn't know any better.

"Stefano, you have a particular talent and passion for hunting werewolves," Dorian said. "No wizard of the College or Castle has captured so many."

"Thank you, High Magus."

"But things have... changed," Dorian went on. "Lilith has re-made and strengthened the Seal of Avalon. Demons can no longer pass through into our world, even when summoned."

"They can't curse anyone," I said.

Dorian nodded. "Only werewolves created before the Seal incident can spread their curse. So far, we've been able to hunt them down faster than they can infect new lycanthropes."

"Yes, High Magus," I said. I was making my own contributions to that, as often and as quickly as I could.

"The Merlinic orders have been aggressively seeking out and dealing with both werewolves and vampires. Denied access to their demonic creators, we can eradicate them from our world. The man you just sent to the Tower was one of few remaining lycanthropes."

I leaned forward across the table. My heart was beating even harder than when I had been staring at Sylvia.

"How few?" I asked.

"*Very* few," answered the High Magus. "But one werewolf in particular is causing us problems in wiping out their curse."

"The Bitch," I guessed.

Dorian's cheeks went red and he coughed into one hand. Sylvia flashed an ironically wolfish grin.

"Yes," she said. "She's been on the prowl for twelve years without being caught, the longest period of infection on record."

Every bounty hunter worth their silver salts knew about the Bitch. The price on her head was the single largest reward offered by the College, short of capturing an actual demon. Which, since demons couldn't cross the Seal of Avalon anymore, officially made the Bitch the biggest payday on the books.

Her true name was something of a mystery – hence the nickname. According to the College's long-posted bounty, the Bitch was believed to have originated in Canada, but had been positively identified all across the world. She had killed seventeen hunters and an unknowable number of uninitiated innocents in the years since her infection.

"The Bitch seems to revel in her curse," said Sylvia. "And worse, she actively spreads it."

I frowned. Lycanthropy was transmitted by bite or claws, but werewolves were wild, brutal monsters. Less than one in twenty victims survived their terrible wounds. But those who did carried their curse and transformed into the very demonic creatures that they had escaped.

"The Bitch kills only about half of her victims," Sylvia said, "creating werewolves at ten times the usual rate. Before the resealing of the Nether, we estimated that the Bitch accounted for nearly a quarter of all lycanthropy cases."

"And now?" I asked.

"One hundred percent."

I stared. "What?"

"The... ahem... Bitch... and her cursed offspring are the last of the werewolves," Dorian explained. "Lilith has confirmed that she senses only a single group of demonic energies matching the lycanthropic curse."

"Where are they?" I asked.

"Russia," Dorian answered.

"I'll be there tomorrow."

"They are the last of their kind," Dorian said. "There will be a substantial bonus for their capture."

"I already said I'm in."

Dorian glanced at Sylvia and she shrugged. They didn't need to tell me how much money was on the line – I didn't care. I would have paid every ounce of gold I've ever earned for one shot at the queen of the demon wolves.

"Lilith would have done this herself, but her baby..." Dorian said.

I smirked at that. Lilith was an extraordinary woman. Her half-succubus blood gave her strength, speed and senses all far beyond human limits. When she fell in love, those powers had only grown more impressive... But I wondered if the challenges of parenting were more than even the great Lilith Quinn could handle.

"Lilith has a husband and a daughter now," I told the High Magus. "I'll take care of the Bitch."

"Very well," said Dorian. "We'll send you to the Castle's eastern keep by portal and provide your target's approximate location. Lilith has narrowed it down as best she can, but werewolves travel swiftly and range widely."

I stood and Sylvia rose, too. She nodded respectfully to Dorian and took my arm, guiding me toward the council chamber door.

"Come with me, Stefano," she said. "We have some details to discuss before you leave."

Chapter
THREE

Sylvia led me back through Dresden Hall, past the ranks of watchful ancient armor and bounty notices, and out into the neatly manicured herb gardens of the College. She guided me past the bronze dome of the observatory and down a winding gravel path toward a small brick cottage covered in thick ivy like green robes.

Only the most important magi of the College had sanctums on the grounds. Since Sylvia had accepted Dorian Vandi's seat on the council, that now included my teacher and I'd be lying if I said that I wasn't proud. When I first met Sylvia, she was a young wizard, still paying off the cost of her training by serving as a bounty hunter. But now she was powerful, both in magic and position.

Of course, I've always been in awe of Sylvia North. She was my savior and my teacher. She showed me everything I know about magic and hunting, about survival. And women.

Sylvia flicked her fingers at the cottage as we approached and smoke began rising from the chimney, warming the little house for her arrival. I waited for Sylvia to speak and expected the conversation to be done by the time we reached her front door. A wizard's sanctum is, for lack of a better term, sacred. It's where we file and organize everything *just so*, where we know the exact location of every herb and chemical, where our magic has seeped into the very bricks and become as much a part of the house as the foundation itself. Inviting someone else inside isn't just a breach of privacy and protocol – unbalancing any of that delicate magical order and tuning, even accidentally, could be disastrous.

But Sylvia remained silent all the way to the cottage and I followed her like an obedient student. Maybe she lived here at the College, I thought, but had decided against keeping the cottage as a sanctum. But I discarded the idea when Sylvia opened the door and gestured me inside.

The air was full of the familiar smells of mockfoil and myrrh, cobalt and the clean, stony scent of quartz. Though to judge by the locked chests stacked in neat towers along the south wall of the living room, Sylvia wasn't quite finished moving in. Properly setting up and organizing a sanctum can take years.

My face went hot. I had just trimmed down my beard after days of inattention in the Louisiana bayou and wondered if it concealed my flush at all. Sylvia wasn't even done making her mark here. Allowing me inside at this delicate stage demonstrated great trust. Or maybe something even more intimate... which only made my cheeks burn hotter.

"Sit," Sylvia told me.

I took a seat at a polished walnut table in the dining room as Sylvia shrugged out of her robes and hung them from an antique coat rack beside the door. She ran her hands over a fitted pencil skirt beneath and then smoothed her cream-colored blouse. Satisfied, Sylvia strode across the cottage, high-heeled pumps tapping out a metronome beat on the tiles. Sylvia's long legs were a hypnotic sight, especially when she sat down next to me.

"Stefano, do you remember when I went after the Bitch?" she asked. "You were young."

"I was twenty-two."

"Young," Sylvia repeated. She smiled a little to soften the word. "Too young and too inexperienced to join me on the job. Even a decade ago, the Bitch had an unparalleled reputation for violence."

"So did you," I said. "You were the best hunter of the College, especially when it came to the wolves."

"You're better than I ever was, Stefano."

I flushed again. Damn it, I was supposed to be badass. I wasn't a lost little boy anymore.

"I never did catch the Bitch," Sylvia went on. "Obviously. But I did learn a few things that you'll need to know."

I leaned forward eagerly. "Tell me."

"Back when I hunted her, the Bitch hadn't been cursed for long. I even managed to dig up some of her origins. She lived in Canada with her family – a husband and three children. Her husband took a logging job, but there was a werewolf in those woods and one day, it tracked him home. He didn't survive. Neither did the children."

"Did the original werewolf kill her family?" I asked. "Or was it the Bitch, after she contracted the curse?"

"I don't know," said Sylvia. "There was a news story at the time that postulated a timber wolf attack."

"Planted by the College?"

Sylvia drummed her fingers on the tabletop and sighed. "Yes. Unfortunately, that was the standard story at the time."

And it probably contributed to the overblown fear of wolves in North America. These days, the College and Castle tried to vary their cover stories when dealing with the aftermath of monster attacks, but innocent wildlife still sometimes takes the blame for supernatural destruction.

"Both the Bitch and her husband were undocumented immigrants," Sylvia said. "So I couldn't find her original name written down anywhere. But Stefano, the Bitch seems to understand her curse. She spreads it purposefully."

"That's... a little difficult to believe," I admitted.

Werewolves were wild and unpredictable beasts, driven utterly by their dark passions. When the demons wanted clever or careful minions, they created vampires. When they wanted mayhem and a high body count, they made werewolves.

Sylvia smiled at me, just a slight curve to her full red lips. "Then you're going to have a very hard time believing the rest of what I have to tell you, Stefano."

I hesitated, but nodded for her to go on. Sylvia was brilliant and much more experienced in every aspect of the magical world than me. I would be an idiot to ignore any information she had to give.

"When the Bitch curses new werewolves, she doesn't let them range out on their own," Sylvia said. "She keeps them close."

"What?" I asked.

"She's created a pack."

A *pack* of werewolves. I've faced dozens of lycanthropes and never backed down, but hunting an organized group of the super-humanly strong and fast demon wolves... I was a seasoned enough hunter to avoid shitting my pants. Barely.

"The Bitch keeps her subordinates whipped into a fury so they can't revert back to their human forms," Sylvia said. "Hunters have managed to pick off one or two members of the pack over the years, but the Bitch always replaces them."

"How many in the pack?" I asked. Most normal wolves gathered in packs of three to fifteen, with frequently fluctuating numbers.

"Four," Sylvia answered. "For a total pack size of five."

Well, that was less than fifteen, at least. It was like being told by my doctor that I was only going to lose half of my limbs.

And I might lose some limbs on this hunt. A single werewolf was trouble. Five was a nightmare. My usual bait-and-trap method wouldn't be easy with that many... if you could ever have called it *easy* in the first place.

"What happened when you hunted the Bitch?" I asked. "You never really talked about it, even afterward."

Sylvia's face was hard, unflinching. "The Bitch was still forming her pack back then, but she's a creature of the Nether. She hated me and wasn't looking to add a Merlinic wizard to her fucked-up little family."

"It must have been bad," I said. "I didn't see you again for almost a year."

"She severed my spine. I only escaped by using the teleportation spell I had set up to send the Bitch to her cell in the Tower. It took three moons to cure the curse and another five months before I could walk again."

Sylvia shifted slightly in her chair and I heard her toes flexing against the smooth patent leather of her shoes, testing the feeling and strength there. I always suspected that Sylvia had contracted lycanthropy, but she never let me visit her during those months of curse-removal and physical therapy. I was six years into my magical training at that point and could manage well enough on my own, but I had missed my teacher.

"I've half a mind to hunt the Bitch myself," Sylvia said. "Payback going by the same name and all. We could take her together."

I shook my head. "You're on the council now. We can't afford to risk you. You taught me well, Sylvia. Let me handle the Bitch."

Sylvia smiled. She slipped one foot and then the other from her high heels, and crossed her long, dark legs. It was a process every inch as fascinating as the most complicated magical ritual. And just as powerful. Sylvia caught me staring and adjusted her glasses. Her smile turned a little sad.

"We used to go to dinner, Stefano," she said. "Every couple of months or so. But it's been three years since we've done more than pass each other in the library. We used to be... close."

Close. That was one way to put it. Another would have been that not long after my eighteenth birthday, Sylvia took my hand and taught me everything I knew about women. She showed me things that I've been able to share with few others – sexual magic isn't exactly a study of the highest priority for the Castle or College, but our order *was* founded by a cambion. Merlin had been Asmodai's son, a half incubus – and if you've read the right sort of books, you know exactly what that means.

The memory of the things Sylvia had taught me sent heat flooding through my body. I drew a deep breath.

"I've been... busy," I said.

The excuse sounded thin, even to me. Sylvia cocked her head and she touched the streak of silver in her hair, then lifted her chin.

"I'm ten years your senior, Stefano," she said. "You've grown up... and so have I. Is that why we haven't had dinner in so long?"

"Gods, no," I answered at once. "You're as gorgeous as ever, Sylvia."

I couldn't get the words out quickly or emphatically enough. My teacher's round breasts strained at the buttons of her blouse and her knee-length skirt was tight across her thighs. The sight made my own pants feel uncomfortably tight, too.

Sylvia brushed her fingertips against my cheek and I barely managed not to groan aloud. I doubted that I was blushing any-more, but only because every drop of blood in my body was racing to my cock.

"I can't complain about how you've grown up, either," Sylvia told me. "I like the beard. Do you remember when I first taught you weather magic?"

"I remember driving to that field," I said. I leaned into Sylvia's touch and closed my eyes. "And then just about creaming my pants when you started taking off your clothes. *Sky-clad*, you called it. Bare to the elements. I couldn't concentrate on the incantation that you were trying to teach me at all... I never have been very good at weather magic."

I could still see Sylvia out in the middle of that grassy field, her arms stretched high over her head and lifting her perfect brown breasts like offerings. I had bent all my teenage will power on trying

– and failing – to watch Sylvia's precise hand gestures instead of staring at her ass. And then trying not to bolt when the time came for me to strip down and go stand beside her...

Sylvia had been so regal, so commanding as she conjured the wind that tugged at her curls and raised tiny goosebumps all across her skin. Now her hand trailed slowly along the rough line of my jaw. It was clenched so hard against any accidental sounds of lust that my teeth were grinding together.

"You don't really have to perform weather magic in the nude, you know," Sylvia told me. "I simply wanted you to see me naked and gauge your level of interest. I never actually told you to get undressed, Stefano."

My eyes snapped open and my jaw fell. Sylvia was right... She had never instructed me to do any of it. I had simply assumed and started dropping clothes into the wind-whipped grass.

"Well, *that* must have been quite the answer," I said. "My cock was as hard as stone and being sky-clad didn't leave me any way to hide it."

"I noticed. And didn't object to the view. All of that training was beginning to build your muscles. You were always a handsome boy, Stefano."

"All of that was just to get in my pants?" I asked.

"Call it what passes for flirting among wizards. It was either that or suggestive comments about your wand."

I laughed. One of the other bounty hunters, Clio, liked to do her job with wind and lightning. But since she didn't hunt in the nude, I assumed that she had learned different spells or figured out a modification that let her keep her clothes on.

I was never as good at weather magic as Clio, but I had conjured up a few storms when the situation called for it. Not often, though... It just wasn't as much fun without Sylvia standing naked beside me.

"Well, it worked," I said. "My first time was right there in that field. Gods, I had no idea what I was doing."

"I showed you."

I put my hand over Sylvia's against my cheek. Surely she felt the heat in my face and noticed the straining tent in my pants. She uncrossed her legs and I caught a flash of bright white silk between them.

"Now, the question is," Sylvia said, "do you remember everything I taught you?"

"Yes," I breathed. "I do."

Sylvia stood and slipped her hand under the hem of her fitted skirt, inching it up until she could hook one finger over the waist of her panties. The sight of pale silk sliding down her dark legs made my mouth water. Keeping her eyes locked on mine, Sylvia stepped out of her underwear and sat on the edge of the table.

"Then come here and show me," she said.

I was out of my seat and down on my knees in an instant. I ran eager hands up Sylvia's legs and my whole body tingled as they parted. It could be hard to tell the difference between attraction and magic. Then again, Lilith Quinn's bond with her husband had given them both supernatural powers far beyond anything the College had ever seen before. So maybe there was no difference.

Sylvia slid one hand into my hair and her fingers tightened. I leaned in between her spread legs, guided by my teacher's firm touch, and trailed my lips along the smooth skin of her inner thigh. Sylvia gasped a little at my kiss and then the sound turned into a contented purr as I ran my tongue slowly up over the soft entrance of her pussy – exactly the way she taught me.

Sylvia was as wet and hot as a tropical storm. I allowed myself a moment to just lick her silky slit and savor the taste. It was tangy and sharp and deliciously slick. I wanted to dive in and devour Sylvia like a starving man, but she had taught me better than that. I traced a careful spiraling pattern in, as precisely as I would have drawn the circle of a spell, and parted her with the tip of my tongue. Sylvia's fingers curled into my hair.

"Yes!" she gasped. "You've been practicing, Stefano."

"You were a good teacher," I said from between her trembling legs. I drew my tongue back up to lightly circle the perfect hard bud of Sylvia's clitoris, but not yet touching it.

"You were always eager to learn," she said. "Every single intimacy spell I knew... Do you remember the first time I cast one? The *Lover's Embrace*?"

I groaned at the memory. Through a conduit of starlight-infused silk thread, the spell linked each partner's physical sensations. When one felt pleasure, their lover felt it, too – simultaneous orgasm, every time. It was a powerful piece of magic, one that almost threatened to overwhelm me at every use.

"I've never seen anyone react so strongly to the *Lover's Embrace*," Sylvia panted. "You were licking me out even as I invoked the spell. Gods, you came even harder than I did."

I drew back just enough to speak, my lips brushing over her slick softness with every word. "It wasn't the spell. That was the first time I had ever gone down on a woman. The first time I had ever brought someone beside myself to orgasm. I was so excited that I just couldn't help it..."

"And that's why you creamed your pants in the volume only such a young and eager man can produce?" Sylvia asked.

"Yes," I admitted.

The confession was shameful, but the rush of excitement was no less even now, over a decade later. Sylvia pulled my head back, fixing her dark eyes on mine. My cock ached and throbbed for release, but I made no move to free or touch myself. I would do only as Sylvia instructed. Slowly, the sorceress smiled and drew me in again.

"Then make me cum," she told me.

The command was almost enough to make me blow right there, untouched on Sylvia's floor, but I wasn't a teenager anymore and managed – with an effort – to keep myself under control. I pressed my lips eagerly against Sylvia's pussy again and slid the tip of my tongue in a swift pattern over her clitoris. Her back arched and the muscles of her thighs bunched.

Sylvia's fingers clenched almost painfully in my hair. She was close... very close. I rolled my tongue in harder, faster strokes over Sylvia's hard little nub and wetness gushed from her pussy.

"Stefano!" she gasped. "Yes!"

I drank in the sound and the taste of Sylvia's pleasure as she writhed on the tabletop until she released me. She panted as I sat back, licking my lips and trying in vain not to search her face for approval. Sylvia's glasses had slipped down her nose and now she pushed them up into place again. Her other hand slid down from my hair and caressed my cheek.

"I really do like the beard," Sylvia said. "It makes your mouth feel at once both gentle and rough."

She pulled me to my feet and kissed me, slow and hard. I closed my eyes. Sylvia had always liked how she tasted on my lips. She pushed me back, leading me out of the kitchen as she licked and devoured every drop of her wetness. By the time I had to stop – breathless and panting from the kiss – we stood beside Sylvia's bed. The sheets and intricate antique quilt were smoothed precisely into place. Not for long, I suspected.

"Undress me," Sylvia said.

I unbuttoned her blouse as quickly as I could without looking like I was hurrying. The buttons were tiny pearls, but Sylvia had taught me to handle spell reagents as minuscule as a single grain of salt, and I was soon sliding the shirt from her shoulders. The soft swells of her breasts were more enticing than any dessert in the white lace of her bra and I longed to bite into them, but that wasn't what Sylvia had told me to do.

I unfastened her bra, dropped it to the floor and took in the sight of her perfectly round breasts, tipped in midnight nipples that made my mouth water. Sylvia pointed and I sank down to one knee to unzip her skirt. I pushed it down her legs and felt my breath coming faster. Sylvia's panties and high heels were already gone, leaving her beautifully, intoxicatingly naked.

"Now yourself," Sylvia instructed.

I yanked my shirt over my head and then kicked away my shoes, pants and boxers as fast as I could. I stood there sky-clad before my teacher, my cock hard and on display for her inspection. Sylvia looked me up and down, tapping her lush lips with one fingernail. Behind her glasses, her eyes were bright.

"Mmm," Sylvia said. "You've kept yourself in excellent shape, Stefano."

"So have you," I answered.

Sylvia's cheeks might have darkened another shade, but then she seized me by one wrist and spun me quickly toward the bed. She pushed me back into the covers and crawled up along my body like a stalking lioness. This wasn't my usual role – I'm a professional hunter, but right now, I was the prey. And I was eager to be caught.

Sylvia trailed her smooth breasts and belly along my aching cock, making me bite back a groan. She straddled my waist and reached down to grab my dick. When Sylvia had me right where she wanted me, she sank her pussy down onto my length and enveloped me in perfect velvet sensation.

This time, I couldn't stop the groan of pleasure. Sylvia gasped, too, and let out an answering moan. She drew a deep breath and flicked her fingers through a succession of intricate gestures so quickly that I could barely track them. A crystal vial on her nightstand suddenly flashed with rosy light.

My dick throbbed in the tight wetness of Sylvia's welcoming body and I wanted so badly to grab her hips, to hammer myself up into her... But I knew better than to interrupt a spell. Especially this spell.

"You keep that handy?" I asked.

"Just in case you ever dropped by."

Sylvia rolled her hips in close, controlled circles as she intoned the arcane syllables of the *Lover's Embrace*. Not that fucking me was a part of the spell, but Sylvia was an experienced wizard and wasn't at all distracted by my cock inside her. I couldn't say the same... I twisted my hands into fists in the quilt as I struggled to be still.

My teacher lifted a long glowing thread of silk from the bottle and wove it through the air. The thread remained floating between us, gleaming with starlight as the spell tied our senses to one another. Sylvia's voice rose in moaning syllables, both the incantation and her body moving over me with rising speed.

The knot of silk tightened and with a final hungry groan, Sylvia unleashed her spell. The thread flared like a tiny nova and then vanished. But it wasn't gone; the pleasure of being gripped inside Sylvia doubled. My nerves sang and I was on fire. I was bursting with sensation, Sylvia's pleasure and mine.

"Now fuck me, Stefano," she said.

Sylvia planted her hands against my chest and rocked her hips urgently, moving my cock deep inside her. Growling, I released the tortured quilt and grabbed Sylvia's tits. They were so soft in my fingers and I felt the hot jolt of her ecstasy as I squeezed them. Sylvia loved it, needed it. I leaned up on one arm, wrapping the other around her waist, and bit into the tawny skin of her breast.

"Yes!" Sylvia hissed.

She dug her heels into my thighs and rode me hard, driving herself relentlessly down onto my dick. I grabbed her ass and pushed myself up into her to meet every thrust. Sylvia's pussy tightened on me, drowning my senses in perfect wet heat. And through the spell that bound us, I felt the burning brand of my cock invading her body, filling her.

I knew how fast Sylvia wanted it and how hard, exactly how she wanted to move, and she knew the same for me. Sylvia pushed me back into her bed and fucked me with expertise that went far beyond mere experience or talent. Every beat of my heart pounded sensation through my body and along my cock. I slid my hands up the hourglass curve of Sylvia's sides and traced her spine with my fingertips, feeling the raised lines of scars where the Bitch had nearly killed the great huntress.

Sylvia's body tensed and bunched as she rode me. She raked her nails down my chest as the pleasure threatened to become too much. Maybe the twin red tracks of pain were supposed to hold us back from the edge, but her primal display of desire only enflamed me. Ecstasy burned through me like wildfire.

"I... I'm cumming...!"

We both groaned it at once. Every muscle in my body clenched and Sylvia squeezed my hips with her powerful thighs, holding me inside her. Heat fountained up from within me and gushed deep into Sylvia, drowning us both in sensation. Sylvia carried me on past the peak and our mingled pleasure kept me cumming so long that my vision swam with colors.

By the time Sylvia finally released me, I could barely breathe. Some women might be used to climaxes that lasted minutes, but few men are and I was out of practice. I collapsed back into the bed and Sylvia remained atop me, smiling in satisfaction.

But she wasn't done with me. I guess that's what I get for not 'stopping by' more often.

"Ready?" Sylvia asked.

"For what?" I panted.

My teacher winked and adjusted her glasses. She lifted her hand from my chest and ran it down hers. Sylvia twisted one hard, dark nipple and I held my breath as my own nerves thrummed in echo. We were still joined by the spell – it didn't matter if neither of us was touching me. She would still make me squirm with pleasure.

Sylvia's hand moved down over the smooth expanse of her stomach and then between her legs. Her pussy was still spread open around my cock and slippery with the creamy cum oozing from where I had shot it deep inside her. She caressed her semen-slicked slit and I gasped at the jolt of helpless ecstasy. Sylvia's smile became a feline grin and she rubbed her dripping fingers over her clitoris.

"Fuck," I groaned.

"We went on so many hunts together," Sylvia said, an edge to her voice as she pleasured herself. She kept her other hand planted on my chest, holding me down. "Tracking werewolves through the Everglades and the jungles. The arctic tundra... The nights there got so cold."

"I remember them being pretty damned hot."

Sylvia moaned and pinched her clitoris, making both our backs arch in a sudden contortion of ecstasy. She tossed her black hair and thick lines of white ran from her still-stuffed pussy, painting nonsense runes across her parted thighs.

"Do you remember the first time that you took my ass?" Sylvia asked.

Fuck yes. My cock throbbed inside her and cum dripped down over my balls in a molten agony of pleasure.

"It was when I finally finished my sanctum," I said breathlessly. "You came over to celebrate with me. It was the first time I had a bed of my own. You said we should do something special to break it in."

Sylvia laughed, making her body ripple and squeeze along my length inside her. I groaned. She rubbed her pussy, filling the bedroom with the wet sounds of fingers moving through the messy load dripping out of her. Sylvia's breasts bounced as her breath came faster.

"Your eyes were so wide when I told you to put your cock up my ass," she said.

"I'd never done it before. I was afraid I would hurt you. I should have known better."

Sylvia's fingers sped and we both gasped at the feeling. I ran my hands over her thighs.

"It didn't hurt," Sylvia said. "I took every inch up my ass and you fucked me with your mouth hanging open the whole time. It was adorable."

"It was amazing," I told her. "And beautiful."

Sylvia spread herself open with two fingers to show off her clit. Covered in the white of my cum, it looked almost like a literal pearl. My fingers curled into the firm curve of Sylvia's ass as the ecstasy built inside us both and then exploded. My cock throbbed in time with the waves convulsing through Sylvia's body and poured more cum into her. There was no room to contain two loads and semen gushed from between Sylvia's legs, down along her thighs and mine. She threw back her head and screamed in pleasure.

At last, Sylvia lifted herself up off of my cock and rolled onto her back in the bed beside me. A freed torrent of cum streamed down her inner thighs. It shone bright white against her dark skin like dripped candle wax. I ran one hand up along her side.

"Candles," I said. "That was something else you showed me."

Sylvia stretched her arms up over her head, pointing her breasts toward the bedroom ceiling. Her nipples were still peaked, even as my teacher struggled to catch her breath.

"Well, we burned a lot of candles in our rituals," Sylvia said. "It seemed like a waste not to use them when the spell was done."

I rolled over to the edge of the bed and grabbed my pants from the floor. Sylvia frowned, but her expression softened when I took my wallet from the back pocket and withdrew a square of carefully folded parchment from inside.

"A passion charm?" Sylvia asked me with a smirk. "That spell takes hours to prepare. Pharmacies sell those little blue pills now, you know."

I snorted. "Not the same thing. You know that – you showed me the spell."

"I needed some help to keep up with a teenage boy," Sylvia admitted. "Gods, you were always worth the effort."

"So are you."

I grinned and unfolded the small square of parchment, inscribed with runes and bathed in the smoke of burning ginseng and mistletoe. Sylvia gave an approving nod at my work and I tore the paper down the center, releasing the spell. The passion charm caught the embers of my lust and fanned them once more up into a bonfire. My flagging dick leapt suddenly into raging hardness and the rush of desire made my heart pound. Sylvia spread her legs slowly, invitingly. I moved between them.

"I've missed you, Stefano," she said.

Chapter
FOUR

Even magical aphrodisiacs don't last forever. After several more hours of ruining her neatly made bed, Sylvia had finally retreated to the bathroom and emerged with a towel. She put one foot up on the edge of the bed and wiped streaks of bright white from her stomach and thighs.

"Stefano?" Sylvia asked.

I jumped with a guilty start. Even after all of these years, I still felt like a schoolboy caught doing something naughty with his hot teacher. It didn't help that Sylvia's full lips were pursed.

"Have you spoken to Dominic?" she asked.

"Dominic?" I repeated. "What? You know him?"

"Yes. He's been assisting a number of wizards here, including me."

Sylvia finished cleaning up and tossed the towel back into her bathroom. She slid into bed again, supporting herself on one elbow to look down at me.

"Dominic doesn't have the mind for magic," Sylvia said. "But he's been helpful. He listens well and he remembers what he's been told. He's young and fit, too – attributes largely wasted in the library and prep labs."

I couldn't stop one of my eyebrows from shooting up. How exactly did Sylvia know about Dominic's level of fitness? Not that I was jealous; Sylvia and I have never been anything like exclusive. And she was a senior wizard of the College. Sylvia could do whatever – or whoever – she wanted.

But... Dominic? The boy was an idiot. A dangerous idiot.

I lay back in Sylvia's bed, crossing my arms behind my head and growled. "Dominic followed me down into Louisiana, just to interfere with my hunt. Nearly got us both killed."

"He managed to track you through a swamp? That's impressive for an untrained man."

"Maybe," I admitted. "But did you miss the part where Dominic just about ruined my entire hunt? And I had to pull eleven leeches off him."

"I did say he was untrained. As you were once, Stefano." Sylvia ran one finger down my chest. "Remember?"

I put my hand on top of hers as it reached the dark line of hair at my navel. "Yes, I remember. But this is different."

Sylvia wasn't so easily deterred. She slid her hand out from beneath mine and reversed its path along my body, moving up across my ribs.

"With some training, Dominic could be an asset to the College," Sylvia said. "And to you."

"To me?" I asked, frowning. "Wait, did *you* put him up to this partner business?"

"It was Dominic's idea, but I didn't try to talk him out of it. He reminds me a lot of you, Stefano. Dominic is young, driven, and very much in need of purpose."

Sylvia's touch lingered over the pale line of a scar on my side. I don't even remember where I got that one. Not a werewolf... I knew all of my werewolf scars. Maybe a yeti? Or a unicorn?

"I gave you direction and training," said Sylvia. "Now Dominic needs guidance."

She caught my gaze and her hard mahogany eyes held me there. Without her, I would have been lost. Sylvia was right – she gave me purpose. She taught me to hunt and help werewolves, to protect a world that had no idea monsters even existed. I might have tried it on my own, but the best-case scenario would have put me in an institution, drugged and ranting about demonic beasts. More likely, I would just be dead.

I owed Sylvia a lot. But taking on Dominic as some sort of partner? I didn't owe *anyone* that much.

"I work alone," I told her.

"Because of your magic?" Sylvia asked. "Dominic isn't a wizard. He has no resonance that can interfere with your spells."

I frowned and tried to think of an answer to that. But Sylvia wasn't done.

"Stefano, you work alone to protect yourself. Because your first encounter with the supernatural world left you an orphan and because you can't bear that kind of loss again."

That wasn't true... Was it? But Sylvia's words made me squeeze my eyes shut against a sudden wave of panic. I still saw my parents there in the darkness. I always did. I smelled their blood, heard their screams and wondered if they would ever stop.

Sylvia's hand was on my chest again, right over my pounding heart. I don't know when she put it there, but her firm touch was enough to help me open my eyes once more and take a few deep breaths. Gradually, my pulse began to slow.

"Stefano," Sylvia said quietly. "You have worked with a team before. You led the other hunters when Asmodai came for his golem. You led them to find Zane Colton when he turned to the demon lord's service."

"Griffith and Muir died on that hunt," I reminded her.

Sylvia traced an intricate star pattern over my chest. "Your hunters found Zane and confronted his master. Leadership doesn't guarantee success. But a lack of it can be devastating."

I remembered. When the College found out that Lilith could open the Seal of Avalon and release demons into our world, High Magus Myrdon sent every hunter in the city to kill her. His own daughter. I had refused the order and the others went without me. The results were... messy.

"And you worked with Lilith Quinn," Sylvia said. "To save Dominic, in fact."

Some of that partnering had been in my motel room bed. The memory of that job was enough to make my exhausted cock stir against my thigh. I shook my head, trying to clear it.

"Those were all extreme circumstances," I said. "Exceptions to the rule. And the rule is that I work alone."

"You worked with me."

"I was learning from you. That's different."

Sylvia settled herself beside me and pillowed her head on my chest. I couldn't see her face as she spoke.

"You have been alone for a long time, Stefano. We haven't seen each other much. You're always on the hunt. Has there been anyone else? Anyone since Bianca?"

A weight dropped in my stomach. It was familiar by now, but it still hurt.

Bianca Taren had been another wizard of the College. Not a hunter, but one willing to swap notes with me, including refining the bedroom spells that Sylvia had taught me. Bianca and I practiced those enchantments more than a few times together... Until she decided to take things to the next level with some other College friends and summoned a succubus. They had managed the complicated spell, but now Bianca was dead because of it.

"We weren't that close," I said shortly.

Sylvia slid her fingers up my chest and then along my jaw. Did she feel how tight it was? Probably. I've never been good at hiding things.

"Perhaps," Sylvia agreed softly. "What about Lilith?"

The hunt for Dominic had been one of my most... memorable encounters with the gorgeous red-haired cambion, but certainly not the only one. Lilith used to call me whenever her own hunts were coming up empty and she needed a lead. It wasn't smart, but I always answered her call. And gods, Lilith always made it worth my time. She was an amazing and powerful woman. And a good friend.

"Lilith is married now," I said. "With a little girl. She's happy and I'm glad."

Sylvia's breath blew warm across my skin. "I know you better than to think you would ever be jealous. But that leaves you alone. Again."

"I work well alone."

"Dominic isn't the only one whose talents are being wasted," Sylvia said. "Ours tends to be a solitary profession, I know, but the Merlinic order exists for a reason. Like the Round Table before us, we have a world to protect. And you're a natural leader, Stefano. The College needs people like you."

"I don't want to lead anyone."

Sylvia craned her neck to look at me, face going hard. I knew that expression well – Sylvia was my teacher and she was about to teach me a lesson. She pushed her glasses up her nose and I knew it was going to be a tough one. I held my breath.

"Stefano, the Bitch and her pack are the last of the werewolves," Sylvia said. "Tracking down and catching them will be the greatest hunt of your life. But if you can teleport them all to the Tower, we will wipe out lycanthropy."

End the werewolf curse. My heart was already racing, but now it threatened to gallop away, entirely out of control. No more werewolves. It was too much to hope for... but Sylvia was right. I would do anything to finish this hunt successfully. *Anything.*

"You're the best werewolf hunter in the world," Sylvia told me. "But you'll need help to catch the Bitch, Stefano."

"Fine," I growled. "I'll take Dominic with me."

Chapter FIVE

The woods were called *Les Krovi*, which meant "blood forest" in Russian. It wasn't the greatest omen to start a hunt, but I trusted Lilith and her strange new ability to detect demons. If she said the Bitch and her pack were out here, then I believed her. Besides, it was nice to be getting some information from Lilith instead of the other way around.

I inspected the forest with a critical eye. Old growth – mostly spruce, fir, pine, aspen and rowan. The last one in particular had useful applications, but they would all help to prevent us from freezing in the cold Russian taiga. Even now, the woods were pale with a frosty rime slowly melting in the clear morning sun. Not much undergrowth, though... That was both a blessing and a curse. It meant that we could move through Les Krovi without making too much noise.

But so could the Bitch.

"Dude!" said Dominic.

The lanky blond stared around Les Krovi, too, though I doubted he was looking at anything useful. His olive-colored eyes were wide and his mouth hung open for a moment before turning to give me a huge grin.

"We just teleported!" Dominic said. "One minute, we were at the College... Or was that the Castle? Dorian said that door was a portal, right?"

Yes, the High Magus had said that. Every Castle and College location was connected by permanent teleportation spells, usually bound to certain doors and keys. It was from the eastern keep of the Castle that I had cast the teleportation to bring us to Les Krovi. I could have done it from my sanctum back home, but shorter teleportations were easier and the Castle was closer to my destination in Russia. I didn't have a chance to explain that, though.

"And then the next minute – poof!" Dominic waved his hands through some sort of gesture that definitely was *not* a part of my spell. "That was seriously cool shit, man!"

"You have been teleported before. I sent you to the Tower."

"Yeah, that pocket dimension where you keep a big-ass magical prison," Dominic said, turning to face me. "Also cool. But I was a raging werewolf at the time. I don't exactly remember the trip."

I heaved my backpack up off the ground and onto my shoulders. Merlinic magic involves a lot of material components, so it makes packing for a hunt a bit of a challenge. At least having Dominic along meant another back to help carry my supplies.

"Werewolves move fast," I said. "We need to pick up their trail. Lilith's lead won't be accurate for long."

At the sound of Lilith's name, Dominic blushed and his grin widened. Remember the part about how she helped me hunt Dominic the first time he contracted the werewolf curse? Well, one of her most important contributions to that job had been distracting Dominic long enough for me to cast my teleportation circle. And being Lilith Quinn, "distracting" Dominic meant fucking his brains out... even after he turned into a nine-foot-tall bipedal demon wolf.

"Right, right," Dominic said, shaking his head. He grabbed the second backpack and swung it up over his shoulder. "Got it. Shit, this thing is heavy. Not that I'm complaining. Thanks for letting me come along, Stefano."

I turned away and began walking. Dominic must have thought I couldn't hear him. He fell into step beside me.

"Thanks, man," he said again.

"It wasn't my idea," I told him.

Dominic's grin turned into a frown, but not for long. I lengthened my stride to pull ahead, but Dominic was a few inches taller than me and matched my pace easily through the trees. We moved swiftly through the fragmented sunlight filtering between interlaced branches.

"Doesn't the Castle have their own hunters for this?" he asked.

"This is *my* job," I answered.

"I'm not doubting your skills, Stefano. I know you're the best. But this is like a super important hunt, right? Do we have backup from the Castle or anything?"

I suppressed a groan. Had Sylvia known Dominic's capacity for questions? Of course she did. Was this supposed to be teaching me something? Patience, perhaps? Or maybe how to murder an ex-barista in the Russian woods...

"The nearest outpost of the Castle is in Bucharest," I told him. "That's where we teleported from. But I wouldn't expect backup from the Castle if anything goes wrong out here."

"Why not?" Dominic asked.

"The Castle has no authority in Russia. They have the power to protect Europe, but this is outside their domain. Other parts of the world have their own magical traditions and their own protectors."

"So it's a... political thing?" Dominic guessed.

I stepped over the winding silver line of a stream and crouched down on the far side to examine a broken sapling. It was a young pine tree, snapped about halfway up its length to expose the heartwood inside. A few black hairs clung to the sap oozing down the damaged wood.

Dominic looked over my shoulder, eyes wide, and reached for the shotgun he carried looped through the straps of his backpack. He waited in tense silence until I stood and shook my head. The hairs were too short and too coarse to be werewolf fur. Probably a black bear.

We kept moving, but to judge by the furrow between Dominic's brows, he hadn't forgotten his question. Eventually, I sighed.

"Yes, there are politics to this," I said. "Complicated ones. There are dozens of magical traditions in this part of the world. Local shamans, mystics and witches; all operating in their own cities and towns. But there's no single organization like the Castle here."

"What about the geomancers?" Dominic asked. "They're just down south in China, right? Do they control the magic here?"

I shook my head. "Their power follows the ley lines and spreads across much of Asia. But not into Russia. They have no more power here than the Castle or College."

"So who protects Russia?"

"Baba Yaga," I said.

"The Russian sorceress?" Dominic asked. "The one with the walking house? With... you know... with chicken legs?"

I didn't slow down at all, but I spared the boy a sidelong glance. Apparently he had been doing more than just dusting the books in the library. Or maybe he had seen it on some television show.

"Baba Yaga isn't just any sorceress," I explained. "She began as one of the local witches, but that was a long time ago. Back when she was still human."

"Then she's not human anymore? What is she now?"

"She's... powerful."

Something moved in the forest, a dark shadow sliding through the tangled shade of Les Krovi. I stopped walking and held my hand out to halt Dominic. He yanked the shotgun from his backpack again and swept the barrel in a swift arc around the swaying pine branches.

A black shape lurched out from between a pair of spruce trees. Dominic dropped down into a crouch and pumped a shell into his shotgun. I grabbed his shoulder.

"Don't shoot!" I hissed.

Dominic tensed in my grip, but he pulled his finger off the trigger. He stared at the bear lumbering through the trees.

"We're carrying a lot of food," Dominic whispered. "Is it going to attack us?"

"Not unless you piss it off. Put that gun away. Even if it were a normal bear, we can't just go around shooting all the wildlife in Russia."

The bear craned its thick, shaggy neck to regard us with milky blue-white eyes, then chuffed a few times and shambled off into the forest once again. When it was gone, Dominic carefully ejected the unused shell from his gun, caught it and replaced the safety. He pushed the weapon back through the loops of his pack and let out a long breath.

"Okay, right. Sorry about that, dude," Dominic said in a shaking voice. "I'm just... Wait, what? Did you say 'if that were a normal bear'? *If?*"

"There are bears out here," I told him. "And there are things that used to be bears."

"What the fuck are they now?"

I didn't have a very good answer to that, so I began hiking again. And for once, Dominic let the question go.

———

We pressed on through the boreal forest, moving more or less northeast in the direction Lilith had given us. There wasn't anything like a trail out here, no hiking paths or roads. We hadn't exactly arrived on a commercial flight or booked a campsite. My teleportation spell had dropped us right in the heart of Les Krovi, far away from any town or even logging roads, and it would take days to reach any sort of civilization.

Dominic followed me through the woods, stepping over stones and roots half buried by fallen leaves. The forest floor began to slant upward under our feet until our hike became something more like a climb. Dominic continued to keep pace, though. Sylvia was right – he was clearly in good physical shape.

But while I might not have been able to criticize Dominic's fitness, the kid was leaving tracks that a Cub Scout could follow and making enough noise to warn everything with ears that we were coming. I slowed down a little.

"Watch your step," I instructed. "Try to keep your feet on the moss or green leaves. Solid stone if you can find it. But stay off dead leaves and sticks. They break every time you settle your weight."

Dominic looked down at the mottled brown and gray leaves at his feet. He nodded and stepped slowly away – right into a fir tree. Boughs snapped against his back.

"And keep out of the branches," I said. "It takes me twelve minutes to inscribe a teleportation circle. A werewolf needs less than twelve seconds to rip us both to pieces."

Dominic cocked his head. "But it takes fourteen minutes to cast the teleportation spell."

"I've been working on my casting time."

"Dude! That's awesome!"

Dominic held up one hand, knuckles out and fingers curled for a fist-bump. I ignored him and moved on. Dominic sighed and resumed following me. He kept his eyes on the ground and actually managed to hike through the woods with considerably less noise. Dominic wasn't going to win any prizes for stealth, but it was an improvement.

The sun sank into the west behind us, turning the slender rays of forest light a deepening amber color. The air grew swiftly cooler, too, and I picked up the speed a little to keep warm.

"So what's the deal with Baba Yaga?" Dominic asked after a while. "She doesn't sound like a very nice lady."

"She's not," I said.

Dominic looked up from his inspection of the ground with eyebrows arched inquisitively. Did the boy *ever* get tired of asking questions?

"The Castle tried for years to establish a keep out in Russia," I explained. "The geomancers were trying to extend their power into the north, too. In the early twentieth century, the High Magus of the Castle and the Grand Magistrate of the geomancers agreed to send out a joint task force to... deal with Baba Yaga. It was the first time our two orders tried to work together."

"What happened?" Dominic asked.

"Ever heard of the Tunguska event?"

Dominic shook his head. "Uh... no?"

"On the thirtieth of June, 1908, an explosion leveled over seven hundred square miles of taiga. None of the wizards or geomancers returned. Now we generally stay away from Russia. And when we *do* come here, we're very, very careful."

Dominic stared around the forest as if Baba Yaga were about to leap out of the trees at him. He reached back to grip the stock of his shotgun and gulped.

"Russia is massive," I told him. "That's a lot of territory to cover."

"But she's got a magic chicken hut," Dominic said, not releasing his gun.

"Baba Yaga lives in a cottage that moves on something like bird legs," I corrected. "But even if the stories of its speed are true, you're underestimating how truly vast Russia is. Our chances of actually encountering Baba Yaga are about one in three million."

"So we just hope she doesn't notice us?"

"I'm not going to pointlessly risk our lives by counting on luck," I said. "Even at those odds. We'll pay our respects and offer tribute. Baba Yaga is powerful and cruel, but she can be appeased."

"Tribute?" Dominic asked. "Uh, what kind of tribute? I didn't bring a lot of money, man."

"We don't need money," I said. "We just need…"

I fell silent and raised my hand, stopping Dominic in his tracks. I drew the silver-loaded revolver from under my left arm and heard Dominic freeing his shotgun again. I motioned for him to remain still and Dominic actually stayed put while I crept forward.

The slope up ahead leveled off into a small clearing carpeted in pine needles. One of the trees at the edge leaned out at an unnatural angle, half smashed into another evergreen. This tree was much larger than the one I had found broken earlier that day, and the bark was slashed open in several places to expose soft pinewood. I inspected the other trees and discovered more claw marks, all thickly crusted with orange sap. The forest floor was dappled in darkened blood.

I measured out the gouges with my fingers. The marks were all long and deep, far too violent to belong to any bear or even a Siberian tiger. But if my measurements were correct – and they usually were – I was looking at the work of at least three distinct sets of claws. Three different werewolves.

The Bitch's pack.

I holstered my gun and whistled. Dominic scrambled up the hill to the clearing, forgetting in an instant everything I had told him about stealth.

"What is it? Oh, shit!" Dominic said when he saw the trees. He clutched his shotgun and whirled, searching.

"There is a lot of sap in the claw marks. They're a day old, at least. But we found the Bitch's trail. We'll camp here tonight."

Dominic put the shotgun away, but didn't remove his backpack. "Isn't it a little early? We can keep going. Really, I'm not tired."

"I have work to do that requires daylight," I said.

"But… here?" he asked.

"Yes."

Dominic took a deep breath and nodded. "Okay, Stefano. You're the boss."

He got to work clearing away the pine needles and digging out a fire pit while I inspected the ruined trees. I prodded at a set of ragged claw marks with my knife, prying up sap and bark. If one of the werewolves had left behind a piece of claw or even some fur, I could perform a divining ritual to see where they would be at noon tomorrow and save myself a lot of tracking.

I discovered nothing but more shattered wood and oozing sap, though. Werewolf claws were much stronger than wood and if they had lost any fur, the wind had long since scattered it through Les Krovi. I wiped my knife clean and sheathed it again.

With that done, I dug a spool of fine-gauge steel wire out of my pack. I left the rest of my supplies in the clearing and walked away from camp to get to work. After half an hour of twisting and placing the wire, I heard Dominic's footsteps behind me, approaching as quietly as he could.

"What are you doing?" he asked in a whisper.

"Setting snares," I answered.

"I packed plenty of food, man. We don't have to eat squirrels."

"This isn't for dinner," I said. "Did you finish with the campsite?"

"Yeah, all done."

I followed him back to camp. Dominic had done a decent job for a city boy. He was used to beach bonfires, I guessed, and hadn't cleared nearly enough space around the fire pit. But the tents weren't going to fall over and Dominic had positioned our backpacks under a small tarp in case of rain. All of my reagents were already sealed in waterproof bags, but a little extra caution was never a bad idea. Soaked herbs and charcoal would make my magic useless. At best.

True to his word, Dominic packed plenty of food. Probably too much, but it was better fare than what I usually brought on a hunt.

Tonight, the sausages and corn were the first to go. Dominic had stored the meat on ice that was just additional weight we could now throw out.

Dominic insisted that it was his duty as my assistant to do the cooking. He burnt his fingers roasting corn and sausages over the fire, but I supposed his beach bonfire practice wasn't a total loss. By the time the sun vanished behind the trees, Dominic had finished with dinner and his fingers were the only things singed. Privately, I had to admit that it was the best meal I had ever eaten in the field.

"You should get some sleep," I said when we finished eating.

"It's still pretty early," Dominic answered. He pulled his cell phone from a pocket of his padded vest and began swiping at the screen. "I've got some studying to do anyway."

"You won't have any reception out here," I warned. I owned a cellular phone, but it was useless until we teleported back to civilization.

"I'm not checking my email or anything," Dominic told me. "I said *studying*. I took some pictures of those claw marks you found. There's a few different sets. Was one of them a bear or a normal wolf or something? Maybe that was a *really* good scratching tree."

I shook my head. "Those marks were all left by werewolves. The cuts are too deep and too far apart to be anything else."

"What about a tiger?" Dominic asked. "Their paws are seriously massive."

"Yes, but tigers have relatively short toes compared to the overall size of their paws. Lycanthropes have proportionally longer fingers – like humans – which often splay when they're attacking and create more widely spaced marks."

Dominic tapped on the screen, mouthing "too wide" and "too deep" as he typed. I don't know a single wizard who uses a smartphone, but I do know the look of an apprentice taking notes.

"Do werewolves have to sharpen their claws?" Dominic asked. "Like cats or something?"

"No," I said.

"Then what was going on here? They sure beat the shit out of that tree, Stefano. Was the pack fighting something?"

I glanced back across the clearing. The campfire lit the broken pines like a battlefield full of shattered weapons. I rubbed my beard and thought about Dominic's question.

"Probably fighting each other," I said at last. "Sylvia told me that the Bitch keeps her pack whipped into a frenzy so they can't revert to their human forms. I think that's what she was doing here."

Dominic followed my gaze, surveying the damage, and whistled. "Wow. She really is a bitch."

The night was growing swiftly cold, but the sky remained clear and glittered with stars, so I retrieved the backpacks from under their tarp. Dominic was typing more notes into his phone, but I had my own work to do.

Merlinic magic isn't a good profession for the disorganized. I usually kept the tools of my trade stored in an assortment of hobby and tackle boxes, but without my truck, transporting two hundred pounds of crated materials would have been cumbersome, to say the least. So for this hunt, I had packed as many components as I could carry into smaller plastic bags and wooden boxes. Any spells I might need still had to be mixed and prepared, though. If we got lucky and encountered the Bitch tomorrow, I had to be ready.

So I moved back from the fire – a lot of spell reagents are flammable or explosive – and began unpacking. I could do a lot of the precise mixing and inscriptions now, leaving the addition of final ingredients or the spoken incantation until the moment of casting. Our magic is intricate and more than a little exacting, but over the last millennium, the Merlinic order has managed to streamline the process a bit.

First, my teleportation spell. The teleportation circle was at the heart of any werewolf hunt and I had cast my last prepared one getting us from Bucharest to Les Krovi. Just as well – once mixed, the myrrh and wormwood were only potent for nineteen to twenty-one hours, depending upon the phase of the moon. I took the granite mortar and pestle from my backpack, briefly consulted a leather-bound volume of my astronomical charts, and got to work.

"What're you making?" Dominic asked.

I didn't stop measuring out the cinquefoil. "Something that requires concentration. Go to sleep. I'll make sure the Bitch doesn't sneak up on us."

"Because you're going to be awake all night preparing spells, right?" he asked.

"Yes."

"Then let me help," said Dominic. "I'll weigh and measure. Just tell me what kind of magic we're working on."

He swiped an app off his phone screen and tapped up a new one. Dominic looked at my spread of reagents, fingers poised over his screen.

"There's no app for magic," I said.

"No, but there are plenty for recipes. It makes keeping track of ingredients way easier. Just replace two teaspoons of vanilla with an ounce of valerian root, a cup of sugar with seven grams of natron, and *bam*! Magic app."

Lilith bought me a smartphone a while ago, preprogrammed with a few numbers and some apps, then presented it to me with a smirk and a joke about dick pics. I still didn't like the device, but at least she stopped teasing me about owning a flip-phone. Even if the phone weren't buried at the bottom of my backpack, I wasn't about to start downloading recipe apps... but if it made Dominic feel useful, maybe he wouldn't get himself killed trying to jump in when it really mattered.

"Fine," I said. "Take notes if you want. The backup scale is in your pack."

Dominic unzipped his backpack and found the extra scale in a wooden box. He smoothed out a patch of dirt, unrolled a piece of foil left over from making dinner, and put the scale in the center. He inspected the brass weights in the case.

"Not digital, of course," Dominic said with a sigh, then quickly held up his hands. "Which is perfectly cool! I can use an analog. So what are we working on?"

"I'm preparing the teleportation spell," I told him. "You can start on some fireballs, if you insist. Do you know how to safely handle brimstone?"

"Sulfur?" Dominic asked. "Yeah. Don't breathe the powdered shit, don't sneeze and be super careful dissolving it into any acids. But I thought you didn't kill werewolves, Stefano."

"I don't, and it takes a lot more than a fireball to kill a lycanthrope. It does, however, distract them. Being on fire tends to have that effect."

Dominic laughed and searched through our packs for the case of sulfur. He found it and opened the seal carefully, then picked a clean steel scoop from another pocket of my backpack.

"Three and five-eighths grams of sulfur for a fireball, right?" Dominic asked.

"Yes," I said.

I heard the note of surprise in my own voice and cleared my throat. Dominic laughed again and selected the appropriate counterweights from the scale case.

"Why are you doing this?" I asked.

"Uh, because you told me to, dude."

I shook my head. "That's not what I meant. Why are you here with me, Dominic? Why are you so damned determined to be my... partner?"

"I tried to tell you already," Dominic said. "Back at the College. Lily saved Max on that island – Avalon or whatever. She saved the *world*. And I helped her do that. I let you guys give me the werewolf curse again to kick some serious demonic ass."

"Do you remember any of it?" I asked.

"No, not really. That ghost, Ben, was in control of my body the whole time. But I know what we did. How can I do something that awesome and then just... stop?"

"Then it has nothing to do with bounty rewards?"

"Nope." Dominic began measuring out the sulfur onto the scale, then glanced back up at me. "Why? How much was I worth as a werewolf?"

"For live capture, just over one and a quarter million dollars."

Dominic's eyes went wide. "Holy shit! Really?"

"Yes."

"That's some serious gold. But you can keep my half on this job. I just want to help do something important. It's not like you're in it for the money, either."

For once, Dominic wasn't asking a question and I didn't answer. He watched me for a moment, then returned to measuring out the brimstone. He added and removed a few yellow grains until the scale sat level, then swept the whole pile onto a fold of paper.

"I'll need two more of those," I said. "And then the saltpeter. You know the measurement?"

"Yeah, I've got it. I don't know how much witchwood, though."

"That depends upon what time of year it was collected," I told Dominic. "I packed a summer harvest, so each fireball requires one and seven-sixteenths of a gram."

"Got it. How much for other times of the year?"

"Two grams for autumn witchwood, two and three-tenths for spring. Anything harvested in winter doesn't work for fire spells."

Dominic nodded and typed all of that into his phone, then went searching for my supply of witchwood. When he found the bag, he snapped a picture of the label for his app.

Preparing fireballs next to a campfire was a good way to earn some burn scars, but Dominic worked carefully and his hands were steady. He mixed the reagents much slower than an experienced hunter would have, but he didn't blow himself up. By the time I finished the mixtures for my teleportation spell, Dominic had three leather sachets set out.

"What now?" he asked.

"They still need to be inscribed and sealed," I said. "I'll take care of that. Go get some sleep."

"And you'll wake me for a shift on watch? To make sure the Bitch doesn't eat us?"

"We'll see."

Dominic stayed awake for another hour, sorting through all of the herbs and chemicals I had packed while I sealed the fireball pouches with beeswax and cinnabar. He asked questions about a few of them and took more pictures with his cell phone. The boy documented everything we had brought and how much of it I used for each spell. When he was done taking notes, Dominic yawned and finally crawled into his tent. Within minutes, I heard snoring from inside.

I inspected our work on the fireball spells for weight and smell. When I was more or less satisfied, I heated a gold-tipped stylus in the fire and painstakingly inscribed an ór rune into each of the red wax seals.

Finished. Each spell would retain its potency for two days and could be ignited with a short incantation. I loaded the fireballs into one of the pouches on my belt with reasonable confidence that they would actually work when I needed them.

A slender crescent moon had risen over Les Krovi and cast thin, pale light through the woods. There were hours yet until dawn – Dominic's help had actually saved me some time, but as the silver moon and stars arced across the night sky, I didn't wake him. I sat silently next to the dying campfire and watched the dark forest for movement.

I've always worked alone. Sylvia pointed out a few instances in which I had hunted with a partner or team, but those times were rare and never lasted very long.

Outside of my job... Well, it wasn't like I had very many friends. There was Sylvia, but she's always been a teacher first, an amazing fuck second, and friend... seventeenth. Bianca and I had fooled around for a couple of years, but then she got involved with infernalists. Summoning demons was forbidden by the College and I supposed that I was lucky we parted ways before that. Dorian Vandi had been my boss first as the administrator of the bounty hunters and now as the High Magus of the College, but I never spoke to him outside those official roles.

Lilith Quinn was probably my only real friend, and the transition from friends with benefits to ones without had been... difficult. Maxwell seemed like a good man, though, and we got along well. Maybe I could count my friends at two.

I rubbed my eyes. That was a pretty pathetic number, even by my low standards. But what else could I expect? I was a monster hunter. Sylvia had trained me in that profession, but I couldn't remain her student forever. I had been alone in the field for twelve years... It was hard to wage a one-man war against lycanthropy and maintain much of a social life.

Dominic would have argued that it was a two-man war now. I snorted and walked out to the edge of the fading firelight to collect several of the broken tree branches. I was more of a baby-sitter than the commander of whatever sort of team Sylvia had in mind.

Natural leader, my ass.

I searched through the fallen branches until I found the ones that I needed: three slender rowan switches. I returned to my seat beside the fire and fed wood into the coal, stoking the flames again. When there was enough light to work without slicing off a finger, I began stripping off twigs, then used my knife to peel away the bark. I cut the two longest boughs in half and shortened the last one to match.

The rest of the night was spent whittling them all down until I had five identical rowan rods. As the sky lightened in the east, I set the wood aside and retrieved five slim white bones from a roll of cloth in my backpack. Yes, human bones. No, I don't murder people or dig up graves to get them. I have a medical teaching credential that let me buy them from cadaver suppliers.

Across the smoking remains of the campfire, the tent zipper slid down and a bleary-looking Dominic crawled out. He straightened and scrubbed his eyes, squinting through the trees. Pale mist rose from the forest floor and swirled in slow eddies around our camp. Dominic scowled.

"What the hell, dude?" he asked. "Why didn't you wake me up?"

"It wasn't necessary," I answered.

"I'm setting an alarm next time. Don't you ever sleep, Stefano?"

"Yes. If you want to help, go check my snares. Do you remember where I set them?" I asked.

"Sure, I can find them."

"There are some bags in the bottom pocket of my backpack," I told Dominic. "If there's anything in the snares, bring it back alive."

"Alive?" he asked. "Right. Whatever you say, boss."

Dominic stretched, yawned a couple of times, and pulled on his boots. He didn't check inside first, but there's no deadly wildlife in Les Krovi that fits in a shoe. So if something came seeking warmth in the night, I could let Dominic learn his lesson the hard way.

He didn't yelp or jump, though, and I was a bit guiltily disappointed. Dominic put on a flannel jacket, grabbed the burlap bags I had indicated and his shotgun, then strode off into the woods.

Maybe there was nothing dangerous in Dominic's shoes, but there were plenty of poisonous things in Les Krovi. And I needed one of them, so I walked a slow spiral out from our camp until I caught sight of something pale in the mist. I crouched and inspected the spray of white flowers: five blossoms, all with delicately fringed petals beaded in glittering drops of dew.

Hellebore. The flowers looked innocuous, but hellebore was deadly shit. Only if I were stupid enough to eat the seeds or roots, though, so I carefully cut free a single small white blossom and carried it back to camp.

You might be asking why I didn't just bring rowan dowels and some dried white hellebore from my own sanctum. I certainly had access to both back home, but they wouldn't do the trick. Merlin designed our magic to be as location-agnostic as possible, but this ritual wasn't one of ours. It came from Russia and both the rowan and hellebore had to, as well.

I arranged the white bones and rowan rods into a five-pointed star, then double- and triple-checked my work. I had performed this ritual only once before and the consequences of not doing it *just* right might be even worse than fumbling one of my own spells.

By the time Dominic returned to camp, the overlapping pentagram pattern of bone and rowan wood was prepared for its special guest star. Dominic cradled a burlap sack carefully in front of him. He set his shotgun down against the rock where I had been sitting and held the bag out to me.

"I'm glad this isn't for breakfast," Dominic said. "This little guy would be good for two bites. Maybe. I'd rather have a protein bar."

I took the sack gently and teased the drawstring open to reveal a small brown wren crouched at the bottom. The bird stared up at me with bright black eyes, wide with terror. I reached inside and closed my fingers around it. The wren squirmed as I pulled it out, tiny heart fluttering against my fingertips.

"So what is he for?" Dominic asked.

"She," I corrected with a sigh. "She's for Baba Yaga. We're in her land and we play by her rules. The Bone Mother has a price and this is it."

Dominic's brow furrowed. "What? Is *she* going to eat it, then?"

"No."

I held the wren between my hands, closed my eyes and chanted in Russian. It's not a language I'm particularly fluent in, so I enunciated carefully as I dedicated the bird's life to Baba Yaga. Then with the final word, I wrapped my fingers around the wren's neck and snapped its delicate spine.

Dominic gasped and I'd be lying if I said something inside me didn't ache at that tiny breaking sound, too. But I knelt and laid the wren in the middle of the star. I set the white hellebore flower on the small, still chest and remained down on one knee, watching. Dominic didn't move, either.

"What are we waiting for?" he whispered.

"To see if Baba Yaga accepts our offering."

The bird twitched and its brown wings flicked out. It convulsed once, twice, and then hopped awkwardly to its feet.

"Fuck!" Dominic shouted.

He grabbed his shotgun and jacked the pump. There was already a shell chambered – probably readied earlier when Dominic ventured out to check the snares – and it flew from the breach, but he was far too frightened to notice. I slapped the barrel away from the bird.

"Don't shoot!" I said.

The wren regarded us with clouded gray eyes, no longer frightened. It fluttered both wings experimentally, then leapt into the air and vanished swiftly into the misty morning.

"What the hell was that?" Dominic cried. "Why did you make a zombie bird?"

"I didn't. I made a sacrifice to Baba Yaga. She accepted it."

"I... what? But that thing got up and flew away, man!"

"Baba Yaga knows what she's doing. She's powerful enough to demand sacrifices, and each offering only makes her more powerful. We just gave Baba Yaga another pair of eyes, another spy in these woods."

Dominic stared at me, then at where the bird had been, and finally lowered his shotgun. "Was the bear yesterday like that? A sacrifice?"

"Probably."

I picked up the hellebore blossom from where it had fallen into the star of bones and rowan wood. The petals were no longer white, but a deep blood red. We had Baba Yaga's permission to be here in Les Krovi, but if we caused too much trouble in her lands, that permission might be revoked.

Dominic fished the unfired shell out of the dirt, brushed it off with shaking fingers and dropped it into his pocket. He forced out an unsteady laugh.

"Price of admission: one bird," said Dominic. "At least it wasn't a baby or anything."

"Not this time."

Dominic froze and stared at me again. "Uh, is that something she does?"

"That bird is Baba Yaga's now. Its body and its life. But a wren has so little of either. A human, though – especially one at the beginning of its life – has so much more to give."

"I can't tell if you're kidding, man," Dominic said.

"The Merlinic order refuses to engage in or contribute to that kind of magic, however." I stood up and slipped the red hellebore into a pocket of my pants. "If Baba Yaga had demanded a human sacrifice, we would have had to track the Bitch through Les Krovi without her blessing."

"That sounds dangerous."

"It is," I said.

"But you really would do it, wouldn't you?" Dominic asked. "You would go after the Bitch even with Baba Yaga breathing down your neck the whole time."

I nodded. "Toss me one of those protein bars. We've got a lot of ground to cover today."

Chapter
SIX

We hiked throughout the day, eating on the move and stopping only when biology necessitated a pause. I spotted a few white-eyed birds and deer sliding silently as shadows through the forest, but none of them intercepted or followed us.

I found more signs of the Bitch and her pack, too: broken trees, deep claw marks and drying blood in spatters across the earth. The werewolves' trail was haphazard and zigzagging, often splitting up into multiple tracks for miles at a time before being reunited and continuing on.

The Bitch was herding her pack and leading them north. She drove them hard, too, as though with a purpose. But what kind of purpose could a werewolf possibly have? Like the wrath demons that cursed them, werewolves were forces of pure chaos and destruction. But the demons were all bound, sealed away in the Nether. There was no way for one of them to be directing the Bitch. So what was going on?

Figuring that out wasn't my job, though. My job was to capture and teleport the werewolves to the Tower. And for that, I needed to catch up to the pack.

"What's wrong?" Dominic asked.

I was crouched next to a shattered fir tree, the wood dark red with more dried blood. Some of the werewolves had deviated from the pack again to kill a Siberian tiger. The black and orange body lay on the far side of the tree, already half stripped by scavengers. Tigers like these were much of why I carried guns in Les Krovi, but they were also critically endangered. Not that the werewolves cared, it seemed. Another good reason to catch and cure them as quickly as possible.

"I need a better way to track the whole pack," I said, standing up again. "Every time we detour to follow one of these... distractions, I'm losing ground. It looks like the Bitch got her subordinates back under control, but how long until there's another split? I don't have time to check every trail."

"Well, we know their general direction, right?" Dominic asked.

"Yes, but the Russian taiga is massive. Even now, we're not traveling quite due north. We're a couple degrees east. If the Bitch is moving a few degrees further off *that*, we might never find her trail again."

"Okay," said Dominic. "So... do we split up when the trail does?"

"Not unless you know how to track."

Dominic shook his head. "Sorry, man. And even if I found anything, I couldn't exactly call you. No cell signal. Now what?"

"Dowsing," I said.

"Like for detecting water? Okay, I'll find a stick. What kind of wood should it be?"

I was a little surprised that he knew what dowsing was, but I grabbed the other man's arm before he could wander off into the forest.

"We don't need a stick," I told Dominic. "It's more complicated than that."

"What? Magic is complicated? Shocking."

Dominic made a face of exaggerated surprise, then smirked at me. His expression slowly collapsed when I didn't smile back.

I unshouldered my backpack and found the properly labeled container. Dominic sat down on the toppled tree and pulled out his cell phone to take notes. I unlatched the box and carefully removed a small bronze pendulum from a bed of earth inside.

"What's that stuff?" Dominic asked.

"Grave dirt," I said. "I'll need some zaffre."

"That's the burnt cobalt, yeah? Right here." Dominic unzipped his backpack and handed me a canister. "What else?"

"Vampire ash and the quartz crystal with the dagaz rune."

I measured out the fine black ash from a reinforced steel container. Dominic offered to do it, but vampire ashes were dangerous as well as a precious commodity – especially now. These ashes were the remains of a vampire killed with a wooden stake through the heart. Both vampires and werewolves had demonic origins, and since the sealing of the Nether, were both dying breeds. But the ash would give my spell the necessary infernal energies. For a while, at least.

Dominic held a small crystal in each hand, staring hard at the runes painted onto their flat faces. I pointed to his left.

"That one is *dagaz*," I said. "It equates roughly to *awareness*."

Dominic nodded and took a picture of the blood-drawn rune – my blood, in case you wanted to know – then handed it to me. While he put the other crystal away, I opened the brass pendulum. I placed the crystal into the hollow center, packed fine blue zaffre and black ash all around it, then sealed it shut.

When I was sure the pendulum was closed up tightly, I drew a deep breath and began the incantation. It would be useless trying to tell you the words of the spell... They're not even words, exactly. It's hard to explain. They are the sound that the universe makes, the squeak of all reality as it spins on its axle, the sound that the rim makes as it rolls across time. Merlin gave us the cipher to make sense of those notes and reproduce some of them, but only if you can hear the song in the first place. Not everyone can.

Dominic couldn't, but he waited patiently until I finished. We stood in silence for a moment and the pendulum began to swing. It arced back toward me and then out ahead, pointing a few degrees east of due north.

"That was awesome," Dominic said. "What now?"

"Follow it. This will guide us toward the nearest demonic power source."

"Really? Is this how you found me the first time?"

"I tried it, yes. But dowsing doesn't work very well in large cities. There are vampires and residual demonic taint left by infernal magic. Lilith Quinn sets it off, as well. I couldn't narrow down the conflicting results."

"Yeah, I get something that points right up toward Lily when she's around, too," Dominic said with a smirk.

I had to agree, but didn't say so. I cleared my throat and nodded to the pendulum.

"This will drain the demonic energies from the ashes," I said. "So we'll need to reload it in thirteen hours."

Dominic looked down at his notes and then swiped over to his recipe app. "You used seven-tenths of a gram of ashes. We've got enough left to cast it eight more times."

He brought up a calculator on the little handheld screen. I had to admit that was a lot of useful tools on a single device.

"That's… let's see… one hundred and seventeen hours of effect," Dominic read off. "That's days of tracking. Should be plenty, right?"

"If we don't waste any of it," I said.

Dominic nodded and we swiftly packed up my magical supplies, then got moving again. In fact, Dominic was nearly sprinting in the direction of the swinging pendulum and I had to remind him to pay attention to his footing.

But we did make good time through that afternoon, following the direct course set by the ash-filled pendulum. It pulled toward the strongest demonic taint, which I hoped was the Bitch herself.

The spell gave me no indication how far behind we might be, but at least we were no longer losing time on dead end tracks.

I kept us hiking for as long as possible, pressing deeper into Les Krovi until the horizon swallowed up the sun. The evening wasn't warm, but the cool air took on a sharp winter edge as it tipped over into true night.

"Maybe we should break for camp," I admitted reluctantly.

"That thing has hours of juice left," Dominic said, pointing to the dowsing pendulum. "And you said not to waste it. Let's keep going. I'm not tired."

He was breathing hard and Dominic's shirt clung to his skin with sweat despite the cold. So did mine, but I had flashlights in my backpack and the reagents for a larger illumination spell if needed. We *could* push on through the night. Dominic was young and if we kept moving, we would get that much closer to the Bitch. And the pendulum still tugged in my hand, straining urgently northeast.

But Dominic abruptly bent nearly double, panting dramatically as he craned his neck to look up at me.

"Actually, Stefano," Dominic said. "I'm really beat. Let's stop for a few hours, okay?"

I scowled. "You're the one who wanted to keep going."

"Sorry, dude. It just hit me all of a sudden."

Dominic was lying and he wasn't very good at it. He *was* tired, but that wasn't why he suddenly wanted to stop. I traced his gaze back to my own hand, the one holding the dowsing pendulum. It was shaking. I tightened my fingers into a fist until they steadied.

"Just for a few hours," Dominic said again, then pointed back down the slope to a small break in the trees. "How about there?"

"Fine," I grunted.

I could have argued. Hell, I probably could have just ordered Dominic to keep going. But tired wizards made mistakes and this hunt was far too important to risk some stupid fumble. Hunting werewolves isn't a sprint – it's a marathon.

So I followed Dominic down to the small forest glade and hung the pendulum from a spruce branch. It swayed there as though in a wind, swinging back and forth. The movement was more erratic than before... Was the Bitch's pack stopping for the night, too? Perhaps circling up around some kill?

Dominic got busy setting up our campsite, starting with the fire and clearing twice as much space around it this time. He worked quickly – not efficiently, not yet, but swiftly. I had to give Dominic points for effort. He might even survive this hunt.

"I need to take a leak," I said.

"Sure," Dominic answered. "Have fun."

I snorted and headed back out through the trees for a little distance. The sun had vanished behind the forest, but some of its light still stained the sky red and violet. I didn't particularly want Dominic watching me take care of business, but my seven-minute walk from camp had less to do with avoiding an audience and more to do with not advertising our presence with unnecessary scents.

Not yet, at least.

I selected a pine tree and unzipped my pants, then did the deed as quickly as possible. The Siberian night was growing darker and colder, so I didn't really want to leave my dick dangling for longer than absolutely necessary. But I still had my cock in my hand when a dark shape bounded out from the trees toward me and I whirled to face the danger.

It was a woman. She appeared to be somewhere in her twenties, maybe three or four years older than Dominic. Her waist-length black hair was pulled back into a long braid – or had been at one point. Now the wild strands that had escaped blew around her face like ribbons. The newcomer was short and slender, nearly fragile-looking. Her dark fatigues and matching shirt, though, were torn violently in a way that was anything but dainty. And through the gashes in her clothes, I saw the shining silver glyphs tattooed all along her arms – the marks of a geomancer.

The girl jerked to a halt just a few feet away, staring at me in wide-eyed shock. Whatever she expected to see, I didn't think it was an American wizard with his dick in his hand.

I moved to stash myself away into my pants again, but the geomancer was already leaping at me. I staggered back, going for a fireball spell instead. The geomancers of China were a major supernatural force in our world long before Merlin was even born. They have historically treated the Castle and the College like children who found their parent's loaded gun, like we're too irresponsible to wield magic. Their disdain usually comes in the form of political maneuvering and snide comments, but there have been a few magical duels between our orders and I really hoped I wasn't in one of those.

This woman was less than half my size – sixteen years of hiking through wilderness and hunting monsters builds a lot of muscle – but force equals mass multiplied by velocity, and she hit me with a *lot* of velocity. We went down together in the sparse underbrush, limbs thrashing. The geomancer pinned my hand, still only halfway to my belt and the spells stored there. She hooked one of my legs with her own and shoved her hips tight against mine.

"What the hell are you doing?" I asked.

"Quiet!" the geomancer hissed.

I pushed, trying to shove her off of me, but she writhed like a snake and held me there on the ground. She might have been much smaller and less physically powerful than me, but this woman was clearly far better trained in close combat. All of her squirming reminded me suddenly and uncomfortably that my cock was bared and trapped between our bodies.

"Let go of me," I said.

The geomancer reached up to slap her hand down over my mouth, but I had already fallen silent. I heard it, too – something else moving through the forest, crunching pine needles and tree branches under heavy feet.

The footsteps were far too loud to be Dominic. Not even that city boy was so noisy. I heard only two paws, not four, and moving too quickly to be a bear on its hind legs.

That was the sound of a werewolf. No wonder the dowsing pendulum was swinging so erratically when I left camp. I should have realized something was wrong, but I was tired and I missed it.

I didn't dare curse aloud, but I badly wanted to. One of the werewolves was out there and I didn't have any of my teleportation re-agents with me. Could I lure it back to camp? But in the twelve minutes it took to cast the spell, the demon wolf could kill all of us. Or infect us with its curse.

The geomancer on top of me whimpered something in Mandarin. I knew the language only a little better than Russian, but well enough to catch the words: *Where is it?*

What was she talking about? The werewolf? Surely she could hear the monster – that was why she was covering my mouth. What else could she be searching for? Before I could figure out how to ask her without making any noise, the earth rose up around us and then closed like a fist, sealing us inside.

But the fist didn't squeeze. The ground simply surrounded and enclosed us, pinning the geomancer tight against me inside. She was hiding us, I realized almost too late. From outside, we would appear to be nothing more than a hump of earth.

Okay, maybe *hump* wasn't the best choice of words... The geomancer who had so abruptly buried us out of sight now lay shaking on top of me in the darkness. Her heart hammered against my chest like it was trying to break free of her ribs and hide inside mine. She panted and gasped quietly in my ear. Her body remained wound around mine, one of my legs clamped between hers. At some point in our wrestling, her torn shirt had been shoved up around her ribs and now my cock was pressing right against her smooth stomach.

I was painfully hard, despite the werewolf outside... or maybe because of it. My heartbeat pounded just as furiously as the geomancer's and hot adrenalin burned through my blood. But if I learned anything from Lilith Quinn, it's that after fight or flight, you can add *fuck* to the list of fear responses.

The geomancer hadn't removed her hand from my lips, so I spoke softly, more mouthing the words than anything else.

"Dominic's still out there," I whispered.

"Who?" she hissed under her breath.

"My... assistant."

The strange woman's lips brushed my ear and she drew a breath to answer, but then something scratched at the mound above us.

"Tā mā de!" the geomancer gasped.

There was another deep scraping sound, then another and another, coming faster and faster. The werewolf outside was digging. It must have heard us, or been able to smell us even through several feet of soil. Lycanthropes had sharp senses and sharper claws. I had no idea how strong the geomancer had made this little bubble of earth, but even if she had somehow crafted it of solid stone, it wouldn't be enough to stand up to a werewolf for long. Within seconds, it was going to reach us.

I tried to snake my hand back down to my spells, or at least to my gun. I had no intention of dying without a fight, but there wasn't room to move. The geomancer girl was trying to do something, too, though I had no idea what. But she had no more maneuvering space than I did and all either of us managed to do was rub our bodies together in the darkness urgently enough to make both of us groan.

The werewolf was nearly on us. I heard its low, bone-rumbling growl. The air under the earth was hot and humid, scented with sweat and... arousal? But then I tasted cold, fresh night air. The werewolf had broken through. Most of my view was blocked by dirt and the woman on top of me, but I could clearly see the twin gold rings of the monster's eyes.

"Shit," I said.

A savage howl cut through the thunder of growling and shifting earth. It was high and clear, edged in a snarl that made me shiver despite the heat of another body close against mine. The barely-visible silhouette of the werewolf jerked upright, listening. That commanding howl came again, echoing across the darkened forest and turning my blood to ice. I had never heard that howl before, but I knew in an instant who it belonged to.

The Bitch.

There was an answering snarl from above us and then the thud of heavy paws moving swiftly away, back toward the Bitch. We lay absolutely still in the crumbling cocoon of earth until the only sound was the soft sigh of wind through the trees. Shaking, the geomancer finally opened her earthen bunker and sat up, hair wild and silver tattoos shining in the faint starlight. She looked down at me with wide, dark eyes.

"Can I put my dick away now?" I asked.

Chapter *SEVEN*

The sun had long since vanished and left Les Krovi in darkness, but I managed to retrace my steps until I picked out the smell of smoke and wet ashes. Dominic must have doused the campfire to hide the light. A good idea, but I made a mental note to tell him to do it with dirt next time. Water created too much smoke. If I could smell the fire, a werewolf would have no trouble tracing the scent back to camp. But that conversation would have to wait. Right now, we had other things to discuss.

Dominic leaned out from behind a pine tree, shotgun braced against his shoulder. The barrel whipped up toward me, but then swung to train on the geomancer next to me. She dropped into a low fighting stance, hands held up as flat as blades.

"Don't shoot!" I said. "Dominic, put that thing away."

Dominic let out a sigh of relief and sagged against the tree. He lowered the gun, but kept his eyes on the newcomer.

"This is the one that you were worried about?" she asked. "Your assistant?"

I winced and wished she hadn't said that where Dominic could hear. Luckily, the boy seemed preoccupied. He held up the dowsing pendulum.

"I heard howling," Dominic said. "And this little thing was going nuts. Werewolves?"

I nodded. "One of them found us, but the Bitch called it away. Are you alright?"

"Yeah, man. Freaked the fuck out, but I'm fine. Is the werewolf gone?"

"Yes. I think the pack is continuing on," I answered. "But they were closer than I thought... Their trail was at least a day old, so they must have doubled back for some reason."

"They were chasing me," said the geomancer. Her voice was ragged and she sounded exhausted.

"Uh... Stefano?" Dominic asked. "You left to take a piss and came back with a hot Japanese girl. What the hell?"

A valid question, I had to admit, and one that I had no answer for. I turned to look at the geomancer, eyebrows raised. Slowly, she relaxed from her fighting stance, though she still watched Dominic warily.

"I'm Chinese," she corrected.

"Shit," said Dominic. "Sorry. What's your name?"

"Jun Zhi. My... my team was hunting a werewolf pack. I wasn't expecting to run across a well-equipped man in the woods."

Jun glanced up at me, then down at the front of my pants. Her high, delicate cheeks darkened and I was pretty damned sure that I was blushing, too. But then Jun gestured around the lightless camp at our backpacks and tents. Dominic tucked the shotgun under his arm and went to the fire pit to scoop out handfuls of wet kindling. The campfire apparently hadn't been burning for very long before he extinguished it.

"Jun Zhi," Dominic repeated as he shook out a clump of damp pine needles. "I know that name. From the quicksilver incident in Cairo?"

The geomancer flushed again, but now her expression became one of embarrassment and anger.

"You could call it an *incident*," she spat. "Or you could call it being held hostage by an arrogant canopic mage."

"You know about that?" I asked Dominic. The politics of the quicksilver trade were way above his metaphorical pay grade.

"I told you, man. I read," he said. "I review all the bounty hunter reports that I can get my hands on. I need to know that stuff if I'm going to help out. And uh... Lily's reports are pretty good... Especially when you don't have a girlfriend."

"Lily?" Jun repeated. "Lily Quinn?"

"You've met her?" I asked the geomancer.

"Ah... yes," Jun said. She blushed harder.

Dominic grinned. "Hell yeah! Us too! What are the odds?"

By *met*, Dominic probably meant *fucked*. The odds were long, but to be fair, Lilith Quinn was a cambion. Her little black book came in more volumes than an encyclopedia.

Dominic balled his ash-smeared hand into a fist and held it out to Jun for a bump, but she just stared blankly at him. I sighed and rubbed my eyes. The last thing we needed to do right now was compare how many times each of us had taken Lilith Quinn to bed. It wasn't a competition.

But if it were... I would have won. Hands down.

Dominic finally dropped his fist and looked to me. "Is it okay to light the fire again?"

I picked up the pendulum from the ground where he had put it and wound the chain around my hand. It pointed firmly northeast once more and shifted only a bit when I moved – just a few degrees of parallax. The werewolves were already far away. Relief unknotted my stomach, but frustration clenched it back up. We would have to close that distance all over again to catch the Bitch...

"Yes," I told Dominic. "Go ahead and light a new fire. But keep it small."

Dominic finished cleaning out the fire pit and then lit another bundle of kindling. The damp logs smoldered and smoked, but he hadn't soaked them too badly and before long, the flames were crackling again and filled our campsite with their dancing orange glow. Dominic sat back on his heels and let out a deep breath.

"So... you two want some dinner?" he asked.

Jun looked uncertain, but I nodded. Dominic washed his hands with a few splashes from a canteen and went to work cooking up some foil-wrapped potatoes. I sat down next to the fire and gestured to Jun.

"Sit," I said. "We need to talk."

"Yes," Jun agreed. "What are you doing in Les Krovi?"

"The same as you," I answered. "Hunting werewolves."

"Only two of you?"

Dominic snorted and waved a bamboo skewer in a very inaccurate approximation of a wand. "This time. Stefano usually does this shit alone."

Jun frowned and I suddenly realized that she probably didn't know who Dominic was talking about. Neither of us had exactly introduced ourselves before she tackled me.

"My name is Stefano Rossi," I said. "I'm a hunter for the College of Merlinic wizards."

"He specializes in werewolves," Dominic added. "No one has caught more of them than Stefano."

Jun looked skeptical at that and I cleared my throat meaningfully with a sidelong glance at Dominic. We were trying to catch a pack of werewolves, not pick up women at a bar. I didn't need an assistant and I *definitely* didn't need a wingman.

"I'm just as surprised to find a geomancer in Les Krovi," I admitted. "And a young one, to judge by your tattoos."

"Because of her tattoos?" Dominic asked. "Uh, look at her *face!*"

"You can't always tell with geomancers," I told him. "The magic that they draw through their tattoos can extend life for hundreds or even thousands of years. Jun could be older than I am."

"Dude, you're like thirty-five. Hardly ancient."

Dominic was off by one year and seventy-eight days, but I let that pass.

"I don't have many tattoos yet," Jun said. "So they could not have altered my lifespan by much. That is what he means."

Dominic squinted at Jun. In the flickering firelight, her silver tattoos flashed through her torn sleeves. Each of them was a square about the size of a postage stamp, made of stacked lines and dashes – the hexagram symbols of the I-Ching, the sacred Chinese book of divination.

Jun rolled up the leg of her ripped pants, displaying another column of shining ink that ran up along her calf. I had seen elder geomancers whose skin was so extensively tattooed that it looked like pages from the I-Ching, every inch covered in the ancient silver symbols.

"So those tats are magical?" Dominic asked. "Neat. What can they do?"

His gaze moved up and down Jun's body, taking in the sight of her slender limbs and exposed skin. It was hard to blame him, but if Dominic pissed her off, Jun was going to tie him into knots and I wasn't sure that I could stop her. Luckily for Dominic, the geomancer didn't seem offended.

"They are not magical, exactly," Jun explained. "Not in the way that I think you mean. Our tattoos only allow us to connect with ley lines, to tie our own meridians and chakras into their flow. That lets us sense and use the ley line's power."

"I understood exactly none of that," said Dominic.

"Ley lines are natural currents of magical energies," I told him. "They're everywhere. Like rivers carry water, ley lines carry magic. Meridians and chakras are the paths and pools of energy through the body. Geomancers use quicksilver in their tattoo ink to bond one to the other."

"Okay," Dominic said. "I get it."

I doubted that.

"Quicksilver is sort of the blood of the earth," said Dominic. "It connects things. Wizards use it all the time to mix things that normally can't be mixed. So the quicksilver in geomancer tattoos help to connect their body to ley lines the same way, right?"

"Yes, actually," I said. He did understand.

"With a thought, you can clench your hand into a fist," Jun said with a nod. "When I have joined my chi to that of a ley line, I can clench land. I can flex the water, or stretch the wind... Depending upon the strength of the ley line and where it flows."

That explained what Jun had been searching for when she was squirming on top of me – a ley line to manipulate. And how she had created the cave around us.

"That is badass," Dominic said.

Jun nodded again and returned to the original subject. "I did not come to Les Krovi alone. Even from Beijing, the magistrates detected warping of the northern ley lines by a demonic presence. So a team was dispatched to deal with the problem. Carefully. We came prepared... Or we thought we did..."

Jun wrapped her arms around her knees and shivered, though she sat closer to the fire than anyone else. Her fingers dug into the torn and dirty cloth of her pants. Jun Zhi may have been a geomancer with magical tattoos and power over the land itself, but she was a werewolf survivor.

I knew that look and part of me wanted to let Jun off the hook, to change the subject and give her time to recover. But I needed to know what had become of Jun's team, what she knew about the Bitch and anything else that would give me any advantage on this hunt. There was more at stake than the pain of one woman, but that didn't stop me from feeling like shit.

"What happened?" I asked.

Blinking, Jun looked up from the fire. She drew a deep breath before answering. "Seven of us left from Beijing. We tracked the demonic taint. Werewolves corrupt ley lines wherever they go, and they were easy to follow. Based on the chi distortion, we expected a powerful werewolf... not five of them."

That wasn't new information, but it was helpful to verify Sylvia's numbers. But no one could have blamed the geomancers for not knowing. Werewolves did *not* run in packs. As far as I knew – and I knew a lot when it came to lycanthropes – the Bitch had created the very first.

And last, if I did my job.

"By the time we understood what we faced, we were already too close," Jun said. "Yazhu gave the order to attack. We moved in as quickly as we could, but the big one warned the others and they fought together. Together!"

Jun's voice broke. She bowed her head and whispered something to herself in Mandarin that I couldn't make out. Dominic held up a small packet of white paper and I nodded. He filled a cup from his canteen and put it next to the fire. Jun lifted her head again and went on in a fragile but steadier voice.

"Yazhu and Mei Li were dead before any of us really saw what was happening. We fought back, but we were outmatched. Shufen tried to rally those who remained. When I was the last, I ran."

The geomancer hung her head again, but couldn't hide the tears caught in her dark lashes, glittering in the firelight. She sat perfectly still for a long moment, then looked up to meet my eye. Her expression was hard.

"I ran," Jun repeated, a little louder this time. "I have been running since dawn yesterday. And the pack chased me."

"That's more familiar lycanthrope behavior," I said. I rubbed my rough chin and felt my frown there. "But there was only one werewolf trying to dig us out of the ground."

"Isn't one enough?" Dominic asked.

"To kill or curse us? Yes," I said. "But that means that the Bitch wasn't driving the whole pack. She called them off... with varying levels of success."

Jun nodded mechanically. "The werewolves were moving fast when we intercepted them. Our attack and the hunt for me... These were only distractions."

"From what?" I wondered aloud.

"I have no answer to that," said Jun. "Perhaps Yazhu knew. But if so, he didn't tell us."

"Cocoa," Dominic announced.

He had poured the hot water into another cup and mixed in a packet of instant chocolate. He held it out to Jun, who regarded the plastic mug skeptically. But she breathed in the sweet smell and finally took the cup, inclining her head slightly toward Dominic in thanks. Jun held the hot chocolate between her hands for a moment before drinking.

Dominic went back to work over the fire, checking the potatoes and then opening a couple cans of soup. He marked them off the inventory tallied on his phone. Jun watched us through the flames.

"I am hardly surprised to find a student of Merlin on the werewolves' trail," she said. "But two of you is unexpected. I thought your kind worked alone. Lily did."

Dominic gave a rueful smile and poured the soup into a bowl that he placed on a stand over the fire. "I'm not a wizard. I'm just following Stefano around to help out."

"He's already been through the lycanthropy curse twice," I said.

"Twice?" Jun asked, frowning. "How?"

I didn't quite understand the question. "We removed the curse, but he got himself infected again."

"On purpose," Dominic added. "Stefano did it that time."

I wouldn't have volunteered that information. It was likely to be... misinterpreted. And Jun certainly seemed to be doing just that. Without turning her back on Dominic, the geomancer shifted to look at me with narrowed, suspicious eyes.

"You try to cure werewolves?" Jun asked. "And then allow them to be cursed again?"

"The second time was a unique circumstance," I said. "But the College removed Dominic's curse both times. He's safe now."

Dominic nodded and flashed Jun two thumbs up, but she was still frowning.

"That seems like a pointless risk," she said.

"At the time, I argued the same point. I... objected... to infecting Dominic again. But Lilith needed his help and–"

"I mean this cure," Jun said.

My mouth snapped shut. Hard. The *cure* was a pointless risk? That cure was the reason for everything in my life.

"Uh... so geomancers don't uncurse people?" Dominic asked.

"No, we do not," said Jun. "How could that be done? A suitably experienced practitioner could take the cursed energies into herself, but then would succeed only in creating a new werewolf."

Dominic scratched his head. "Yeah, I can see the problem."

"Then what do geomancers do with werewolves?" I asked. Both Jun and Dominic jumped at the snarl in my voice. "What would you have done to the Bitch and her pack?"

"Usually we trap demon wolves in the earth," Jun answered. "Deep underground. Even a werewolf must breathe. Or they can be killed with the silver horn of a qilin."

"Qilin?" Dominic asked. "Isn't that a Chinese unicorn?"

Jun sniffed. "Both have horns, yes, but unicorns are just magical goats. Qilin are different creatures entirely, great spirits of purity. They are far more rare and far more powerful."

Dominic grabbed his cell phone, nodding and taking notes. Jun looked through the flying embers of the campfire, up toward the sky. Her expression finally softened a little and she even smiled faintly.

"I saw a qilin once, when I was a girl. She had golden scales and a mane like the clouds. She was so beautiful," Jun said, then shook herself out of her reverie. "Yazhu brought a qilin horn from Beijing for this hunt."

"What happened to it?" Dominic asked. "Maybe we can get it back. We could sure use some more anti-werewolf weapons."

I stood and crossed my arms. "No, absolutely not. Dominic, this is my hunt and you agreed to follow my orders. Those werewolves are human beings. They didn't ask to become monsters and we're not killing them. Not with silver or a qilin horn."

"Sure, Stefano," Dominic said. "You're the boss."

Jun shook her head at me, strands of inky hair brushing her cheeks. "You are a strange man."

"Perhaps," I agreed. I had certainly been called worse. "What if someone from your team survived? Would you really rather see them dead than try a cure?"

Jun narrowed dark eyes at me, though her hands trembled. "No one survived. No one."

I sighed and rubbed one temple. That hadn't made my point quite the way I wanted it to. But it also made sense. Only four percent of werewolf victims survived to carry on the curse. Those numbers were even lower among College bounty hunters. Lycanthropes displayed an instinctive hatred of Merlinic magic and few wizards walked – or limped – away from encounters with them. Sylvia had lived, but only because she managed to teleport to the Tower before the Bitch could kill her.

"It was like she knew," Jun said quietly, as though speaking to herself.

"Knew what?" I asked.

"That we were trying to stop her pack. Even if we didn't know from what."

"Were you hurt?" I asked.

"I am a trained geomancer," Jun told me. "I can make my skin as hard as metal. Care to test me?"

"Werewolves can tear metal. I need to know if you're infected."

Jun's dark eyes widened, then narrowed again. Her jaw clenched and she held my gaze for a long moment, but then finally nodded shortly and climbed to her feet. I felt like an asshole, but this was important.

"Dominic, take a flashlight and the pendulum," I said. "Go walk the perimeter. Make sure the Bitch is still moving the same direction. If they changed heading at all–"

"Haul ass back here and let you know," Dominic finished. "Got it, boss. Just keep an eye on dinner. I don't want it to burn."

Dominic selected a flashlight from his backpack, then took the bronze pendulum and his shotgun. He juggled them for a second before finding an arrangement that allowed him to carry all three, and then headed out into the forest. When Dominic was outside the circle of firelight, I returned my attention to Jun.

"I'm sorry about this," I said. "But I need you to take off your clothes."

The clenched jaw returned, along with a fiercely jutting chin, but there was understanding in Jun's eyes. I knew she would have demanded the same thing in my place and briefly considered the benefits of reciprocating.

As a gesture of trust. Get your mind out of the gutter.

Jun grabbed the hem of her shirt. It had probably been a warm, utilitarian garment once, but now it was little more than a tangle of black rags. She pulled it up over her head in a single fluid motion and I couldn't help noticing that she wasn't wearing anything at all beneath. Jun's small breasts were peaked, nipples hardened by the cold night despite how close she stood to the fire. At least, I *assumed* it was the cold...

Jun hooked her thumbs through the waist of her pants and then shoved them down around her ankles with another quick movement. A pair of lacy blue panties followed suit so swiftly that I wondered if Jun was trying to hide them, and left her naked in front of me.

"Are you just going to stare?" she asked.

Right. To business.

I inspected her body by the firelight, instructing Jun to lift her tattooed arms so that I could check for the scratch of even a single werewolf claw. Nothing.

"Turn around, please," I said.

Jun pivoted on the balls of her feet and swept her long black disheveled braid away over one shoulder. She held out her arms like a dancer for my scrutiny. A single column of quicksilver tattoos ran down the delicate curve of her spine, shining there like patches of moonlight.

The sight of the naked young geomancer was enough to send heat rushing between my legs and tent my pants. But I gritted my teeth and examined Jun's back from her shoulders all the way down to her smooth ass.

Jun was trembling by the time I moved my inspection along her legs, goosebumps breaking out across her skin. There were a few streaks of dirt and the dark blooms of several bruises, but I could find no lacerations anywhere on the geomancer's lithe body. Jun's ruined clothes seemed to be the result of her flight through Les Krovi, not the claws or fangs of a werewolf.

"You can get dressed," I said.

Jun yanked her pants back up and I retrieved her shirt from the ground, offering it to her. The geomancer's fingers brushed mine as she took it.

"Satisfied?" Jun asked.

No...

She was still holding her shirt, giving me an all too tempting view of her breasts and the soft hollow of her navel. I hoped that the shadows would hide the bulge in my pants.

"You're fine," I said instead. "But I had to check."

Jun pulled her shirt down over her head, then smoothed it into place. She shook out her wild black hair and nodded.

"I understand," Jun said. "It is not unknown for victims to lie about their curse."

When the price was death – either by being sealed away in the earth or run through with a qilin horn – I could see why. Though I sure as hell never would have done anything like that to Jun, I appreciated her understanding. And her clothes, as she put them back on... It was a lot easier to think with more blood in my brain and less in my dick.

Footsteps crunched out in the forest, but were followed by the bright beam of a flashlight. The light turned off as Dominic trotted back into camp. He nodded toward Jun.

"All clear?" he asked.

"Yes," I said. "She's not infected."

Dominic set down his shotgun and held up the pendulum. "I walked a full circle, about fifty yards out. The thingy pulled pretty much the same direction the whole time. Not real hard, though. I think the Bitch is getting further away."

I couldn't help a low growl of frustration and Jun darted a look at me. I would have to pick up the Bitch's trail again in the morning and work hard to close in on her pack. Tomorrow was going to be a long day.

Dominic rehung the pendulum on a tree branch and finished making dinner. I had entirely forgotten about the food while I inspected Jun. Luckily, Dominic hadn't been gone long enough for anything to burn. He pulled the potatoes out of the fire, poured the now-hot soup into large plastic mugs and handed out dinner. We ate swiftly and silently.

At least until Dominic started asking questions. Again.

"So I read about you in Lily's report," said Dominic, cocking his head toward Jun. "It wasn't super detailed or anything – I don't think she gives reports at all unless the High Magus nags her about it. But I was wondering about something."

"What is it?" Jun asked.

"You were Ptah's hostage, right?"

Jun nodded. "One of many, yes."

"But geomancers are obviously pretty badass. I mean, you came out here to kill werewolves. So why didn't you just... I don't know... magic your way out of Ptah's palace? How the hell did that asshole keep you prisoner?"

"Dominic," I warned.

Jun was frowning deeply, but she shook her head and waved me off.

"Lily did not understand, either," Jun answered. "I was younger then. I was an apprentice when Ptah demanded me as a hostage. Meaning that I had none of my tattoos yet."

"So... no magic?" Dominic asked.

"Less magic," Jun said. "I could marshal my own chi, but not yet affect any energy outside my body. I was not without magic, and I was trained to fight. Ptah's guards would have been hard pressed to prevent me from escaping."

Dominic cocked his head curiously. "Then why didn't you make a run for it?"

"Ptah controls the only font of quicksilver left in the world," Jun explained, touching one of her gleaming tattoos through her torn shirt. "If I escaped, Ptah would have been furious. He might have raised the cost of his quicksilver higher than we could pay, or refused to sell it at all."

"That... sucks," said Dominic. He was starting to look like he regretted asking.

"We needed quicksilver," Jun told him. "So we paid the price."

I stood and collected the dishes from around the fire. "Dominic, go get some sleep. I'll keep a watch."

"Promise you'll get me up for a turn this time?" he asked.

The Bitch was traveling northeast again, with some purpose even more powerful than the urge to hunt Jun. The chances of her werewolves backtracking to find us now were remote and I was exhausted.

"Yes," I told Dominic. "I'll wake you in a few hours."

The boy grinned and punched the air like I had just promised to buy him an expensive car. Jun looked confused at Dominic's enthusiasm.

"You can have my tent," I told the geomancer. "I can hot-bunk with Dominic."

Her brow furrowed. "Oh, are you two...?"

"No," I said. "Hot-bunking just means I'll sleep in Dominic's tent while he's on watch."

Jun regarded me for a moment and then shook her head. "Many thanks, but I will decline. I need time to meditate. I haven't been able to for days."

"Suit yourself," I said.

Jun shifted beside the fire, crossing her legs and straightening her spine. She rested her hands on her knees, fingers spread and palms up, then closed her eyes and released her breath in a long, soft hiss.

She sat that way, unmoving as a statue, while Dominic crawled into his tent and I cleaned up after dinner. Jun's eyes stayed shut as I scrubbed out the dishes and then unpacked my spells to check over each component. She seemed quite capable of blocking out every distraction, ignoring the creaking of Les Krovi all around us as the cold wind pushed and pulled at the trees.

A log on the fire popped and collapsed, throwing an expanding bloom of embers up into the darkness, but Jun remained motionless. I watched her and had to admit that I thought it was a trick of the firelight at first. Bruises I had noted during my earlier inspection were rapidly fading, turning into faint yellow splotches across her skin and then vanishing entirely. I knew a healing spell, but it required a lot more time and preparation than Jun's meditation.

Impressive.

Jun had her magic to do, and I had mine. I collected the demon-dowsing pendulum from its branch and felt the weight. It didn't need to be repacked yet, but it would by morning.

So I retrieved the vampire ash and zaffre from my pack, but found enough of both already measured out in small plastic bags. I wasn't sure when Dominic had done that and I double-checked his work, but the weights were correct and probably already marked down in his phone somewhere. That didn't leave me much to do except watch the pendulum swing back and forth, toward me and then out in the direction of the Bitch. The pendulum wobbled occasionally – making my heart race each time – but always resumed its northeastern arc.

Keeping a werewolf pack moving together was obviously difficult, though the Bitch was just as obviously managing it. But why?

I didn't sit as still as Jun, but I remained silent while I scanned the night for movement. The only sound was the wind in the trees, though, punctuated by the snap of the fire and burnt wood settling. I woke Dominic at three in the morning with instructions to get me up when the sun rose.

"Sure, dude," he whispered. "Now get some rest."

I climbed into my tent and lay down. Sleep came quickly for me and I dreamed of demonic golden eyes in the darkness.

Chapter EIGHT

I woke to the sound of Dominic's voice and the smell of instant coffee. I sat up and squinted at the silhouette standing outside my tent, backlit by the morning sun.

"Sorry, man," said Dominic. "It's hard to knock on a tent."

"What time is it?" I asked.

"About seven o'clock. We let you sleep in a little."

"What?" I snarled.

Dominic backed out of the flap of my tent and I followed him into the cold Russian morning. My assistant raised his hands.

"It's not like we were going to leave before eating breakfast," Dominic said. "Right? I just let you sleep while I was cooking. We're not losing any time."

Jun was seated on the other side of the ashy gray remains of last night's campfire, drinking what smelled like some more hot chocolate. The geomancer's dark eyes glittered, but the cup hid the rest of her expression and she didn't say anything. I growled and ran one hand through my hair. It was tangled from sleep and caught in my fingers. This is exactly why I don't let my beard get long. The hair on top of my head is trouble enough, thanks.

"Fine," I sighed. "But I want to be done and packed in twenty minutes."

"Got it," said Dominic.

I turned to Jun. "And when we're finished with breakfast, I'm teleporting you back to Beijing."

Jun set down her mug, revealing a deep frown. "What?"

"You lost your team," I said. "You've done enough. Your hunt is over and it's time to go home."

Jun stood, putting her hands on her hips. Strands of black hair framed her pretty face and did absolutely nothing to soften the stony look of resolve there.

"Thank you for sharing your food and your fire," Jun said in a tight voice. "But I am not going home yet. There are several small ley lines nearby. I have borrowed enough of their power to resume my hunt."

The geomancer inclined her head and began to turn away, but I grabbed her shoulder.

"The Bitch and her pack killed six geomancers," I reminded Jun. "You barely escaped with your life."

"I have a job to do."

My hand tightened on her shoulder. "You'll die doing it."

"Werewolves are dangerous and a plague upon this world," Jun said. Her voice shook a little. "It is my duty and my honor to die fighting them, if I must."

"Stefano...?" Dominic said.

I waved him away and released Jun. She wasn't overstating the threat of lycanthropy and I had no right to stop her from trying to hunt them, but...

"The Bitch will kill you," I said. "And you want to kill her. It's *my* job to keep both of those things from happening."

"Then it seems that we have reached an impasse," Jun agreed. She settled back into a fighting stance. "I must complete my hunt, but you cannot let me."

"Stefano," Dominic repeated.

"Get out of the way," I said.

One of my hands fell to my belt and the spells prepared there. What, you think I took it off when I slept? Think again. Jun saw my movement and nodded grimly.

"Stefano!" Dominic shouted. He jumped in front of me, waving his arms. "Dude, what the hell are you doing?"

"Settling this," I said.

"Uh... don't you two ever watch cartoons?" Dominic asked.

Jun and I stared. What the hell was he talking about? Dominic caught our looks of confusion and sighed.

"Jun, your team is gone," he said. "And Stefano, we are seriously outnumbered. We could really use some extra help. If you two *ever* watched television, you would totally know it's time to team up."

Team up...? I was already managing Dominic, trying to keep the boy safe and out from underfoot. Now he wanted to add the geomancer into this unstable mix? But Jun was nodding.

"I have never worked with a Merlinic wizard before," she said. "But you say that you're an expert. Perhaps you deserve a chance to prove it."

"I said nothing of the sort," I pointed out stiffly. "Dominic did."

Dominic gave me what I guessed was supposed to be a stern look, but which was closer to puppy-dog eyes. Jun's gaze was more like onyx, hard and bright. Great. First Dominic and now Jun.

"Fine." I crossed my arms. "But we do this *my* way. We're taking them all alive."

"Very well," Jun said. "Until the werewolves threaten innocent human lives. Then I will do everything in my power to stop them."

"Stefano won't let that happen," Dominic assured her. "This is going to be great!"

"Fifteen minutes until we break camp," I said.

"Hey, what happened to twenty?" Dominic complained.

"Ten minutes!"

———

After a quick meal of oatmeal and several cups of coffee, Dominic and I cleaned up camp in just over twelve minutes. Jun had nothing to pack and when we offered her some fresh clothes, the geomancer shook her head. She seemed perfectly fine without a coat or even an intact shirt. Jun probably would have been comfortable in shorts and a t-shirt. Or naked.

I tried not to think about that too much.

We followed my dowsing pendulum as the sun rose and banished the pale tendrils of mist. The trail continued to wander as the Bitch's pack was driven by their demonic passions, chasing after whatever they saw or smelled. But it always evened out as the Bitch hounded them back onto course.

After two hours, the pendulum's arc slowed and then abruptly stopped. The ashes inside were depleted. Dominic halted beneath an aspen tree and unzipped his backpack.

"I've got the next batch ready to go," he said.

I unsealed the pendulum and emptied its contents into a silver-lined box. Even drained vampire ashes aren't something that responsible wizards just dump out on the ground. The quartz crystal inside the pendulum was blank and clear again, the red rune faded from use.

Dominic tossed me the little plastic bags that contained the pre-measured reagents I had noticed the night before and held out a new quartz crystal. It was already painted delicately in blood with the red dagaz rune. I inspected the inscribed crystal, then looked at Dominic.

"You did this?" I asked.

"Yeah," he said, nodding. "Is it right? I copied it exactly from the picture."

Dominic held up his cell phone and I spotted the nick on his thumb where he must have cut it for the blood.

"It looks correct," I told him. "But next time, cut the back of your hand or your arm for the blood. Injured fingers make for clumsy hands."

Dominic grinned. "Sounds like something Sylvia would say."

"Where do you think I learned it?"

I placed the new crystal into the pendulum, then began carefully pressing the ash and zaffre in around it. I glanced up at Jun, who was watching the process with obvious curiosity.

"You told us that the geomancers detected the Bitch's demonic taint from Beijing," I said. "Is that how you tracked the pack?"

"Yes," Jun answered. "The chi distortion of five werewolves is considerable."

"Can you follow them?" I asked.

Jun had borrowed a comb from Dominic to untangle and then rebraid her long raven hair into a single rope. Now it danced across her shoulders as Jun shook her head.

"Not at this distance," she said. "I am no master. When we get closer, I will be able to sense the werewolves more clearly."

Then we still required the dowsing pendulum. I nodded and sealed up the bronze capsule, then closed my eyes and spoke the incantation. The pendulum began to swing, pointing the way northeast.

We set off through Les Krovi once more, moving quickly. By midmorning, both Dominic and I were streaming with sweat. Jun was at least six inches shorter than me and had to take three steps for every two of mine, but she had no trouble keeping up. In fact, the geomancer didn't even seem to tire. The power Jun had taken from the ley line that morning was serving her well.

I was familiar with the geomancers and the theory of their magic, of course. But I had never met one before, let alone worked closely with them. Most of the Merlinic wizards who had partnered with geomancers died at Tunguska and weren't available to share their experiences. I tried to view this impromptu partnership as an opportunity to observe and study... but mostly I just wondered how I ended up with two people following me through the Russian taiga and when my life would finally return to normal.

"Stefano?" Jun asked.

I glanced up from the pendulum and around the woods for danger, but saw only trees and bushes in every direction.

"What is it?" I asked.

"You intend to take the werewolves alive," she said.

"That's right."

"How?" Jun asked. "Will you cure them here, in the forest?"

"No. I'll bait the lycanthropes and get their attention, then lure them in close enough to teleport to the Tower."

"That's a magical mini-reality where the College keeps a super cool prison," Dominic explained. "There are silver cages to hold the werewolves while the wizards cure them."

"And you can do this to the entire pack?" Jun asked.

I considered that. My usual bait-and-switch tactics worked well enough for single targets, but five werewolves would complicate things. I had spent every moment since arriving in Les Krovi trying to find the Bitch and not much time thinking about how to deal with her pack when I did.

Teleport them, certainly... But I doubted my spell could transport five raging lycanthropes, even if we could get all of them into the circle at once.

"No," I admitted. "I can only reliably teleport one werewolf at a time. We'll need to separate the Bitch's pack."

"Why do you call her that?" Jun asked me.

"The Bitch?"

Dominic snickered. "You should see a room full of bearded old wizard dudes talking about her. I swear I can hear their assholes clenching up every time they have to say it."

"We don't know her true name," I told Jun. "Before she was cursed, she and her family had immigrated illegally to Canada. So there's no formal documentation. She is, however, a female canine. So *the Bitch* is as proper a name for her as any."

"Good," Jun said with a small, hard smile. "That's what I was going to call her anyway."

Dominic's snicker turned into loud laughter. Jun was half a step behind me and I hoped she couldn't see me smirking, too.

The geomancer moved as quietly as a falling leaf and I wondered if Dominic was taking notes. But Jun's silence meant that I didn't immediately realize that she had stopped. After a few paces, though, I glanced back at her. Jun was staring off to one side with a frown on her lips. Could some of the werewolves have broken ranks to chase her again? But no, the pendulum wrapped around my hand was still swinging out to the northeast.

"What is it?" I asked.

"Dryad," Jun said.

"Shit. You can sense her?"

"Yes," Jun said. "Fae have a more subtle effect on ley lines than werewolves, but she is very close."

"And she's in our way?" I asked.

Jun nodded gravely.

"Wait, hang on a minute," Dominic interrupted. "Dryads are Seelie fairies. Good guys, right? Why are we worried about this?"

"Because Seelie doesn't mean harmless," I answered. "Dryads are playful and if we get caught in her games, we could be stuck wandering circles in her part of the forest for days. Or weeks. And if we anger her, a dryad can make our lives very difficult."

"What, like she could turn us all into squirrels or something?" Dominic asked.

I crouched down, letting the pendulum swing idly between my knees as I thought. Could we go around? Jun sensed the fairy's domain, but even a single dryad's territory could be hundreds of acres. Circumnavigating that might cost us even more time than going through.

"Uh... nobody is saying *no*," Dominic protested. "Squirrels? Seriously?"

"We do not let fairies roam wild in our lands," said Jun. "There is an order to the world and we require even the fae to uphold that order. They are guests in our realm, after all."

I picked up some pine needles and rubbed them between my fingers, shaking my head. "The Lady of the Lake always counseled a more hands-off approach to the Castle and College. Other than a few particularly problematic Unseelie, we generally leave the fae to their own devices."

"The Mistress of Many Waters did not visit our courts often," Jun said carefully. "She showed the wizards particular favor."

I glanced at Jun, eyebrow raised. Was she saying that the geomancers were jealous of Evaine's visits to the College and Castle? If so, I couldn't blame her one bit. I had only met the Lady of the Lake a few times, but I mourned along with the rest of the Merlinic order when she was killed. Evaine had been a great woman.

"Hey, maybe this dryad is good news," said Dominic. "Won't she play tricks on the Bitch, too? Like use crazy fairy magic to make the pack all drunk or dance for days? Maybe we can sneak up on some dancing werewolves and *bam!* We can teleport their furry asses right to the Tower."

At least he didn't suggest trying to add a dryad to our party, too. My hands were already more than full.

"Only a mad dryad would interfere with werewolves," Jun said.

"Why not?" Dominic asked.

"Demons are the most powerful supernatural force in any of the worlds," I answered. "Do you think they stopped at Earth? Before Merlin created the Seal of Avalon, the demons conquered fairies and djinni and just about everyone else. Even the spirits and the Unseelie fae bowed down to the demon lords."

"But the demons are all gone," Dominic argued. "Lily locked them up in the Nether, right?"

"Yes, but werewolves are still demonic creatures," I told him. "It takes more than magic pollen and conjured vines to stop one. But three humans..."

"Play time," Dominic finished. He stared out into the shadowed forest. "Right. So what do we do now?"

I brushed my hands clean and stood again. "We're not giving up the hunt and don't have time to go around. We need to find the dryad and negotiate for safe passage through her territory."

"It's... uh... not going to be like the offering to Baba Yaga, is it?" Dominic asked. He looked a little queasy at the idea.

"No," I said. "But the price may still be high. Jun, can you take us to the dryad?"

She nodded. "I can. Are you certain you wish to seek her out? Dryads can be wild creatures."

"I don't see any other choice," I said. "Lead on."

Jun led us through the woods, between trees that grew close and whose trunks were soft with thick moss. Les Krovi was changing subtly as we moved deeper into the dryad's territory. The leaves and needles of the forest were so vibrantly green that they almost seemed to glow. Scents of sweet sap and wet earth flowed together into a rich perfume. The wind blowing through the trees whispered seductively in my ear with a voice I couldn't quite make out.

Jun paused occasionally, examining something in the apparently empty air. The ley lines, I assumed. Just as Merlin taught the wizards to listen to the sounds of creation, the geomancers studied the threads that stitched it all together. Each time, Jun seemed to find what she was looking for and urged us onward.

The trees were different here. There hadn't been many cedar trees in Les Krovi, far outnumbered by spruce, pine and fir. But now I was surrounded by the red-brown of their bark and delicate green needles tugged at my hair and clothes. The bright, heady smell of sun-warmed cedar filled my senses, waking memories the way only scent can.

My first time seeing Sylvia naked, her arms raised to the sky. My pulse pounding, blood hot with desire and youthful hormones.

Bianca Taren staring over her shoulder at me, grinning with wicked desire as she told me to fuck her hard. Harder!

The first time Lilith cornered me just outside Dresden Hall. Her red, red hair was like flame pouring down her back. Asking for a lead, a tip on her hunt. And then Lilith sinking slowly to her knees with a wink and an invitation for my tip...

Pressed face to face, body to trembling body against Jun in the darkness of the shelter she had created to hide us. Her breath coming fast and hard, warm on my cheek. The geomancer standing naked in the firelight, her skin shining golden and her tattoos silver. Jun's wild hair, wishing I could sink my fingers into it and pull her close...

I staggered and had to steady myself on the nearest tree, squeezing my eyes shut against the onslaught of memories. When I looked up again, we were no longer alone in the woods. I found myself staring at a very beautiful, very naked woman with pale green skin and long hair the deep red-brown color of cedar wood.

Beside me, Dominic had unstrapped his shotgun and was raising it slowly toward the dryad, moving with dreamy lassitude.

"No, don't shoot," I said. "Put that thing away!"

Dominic lowered his weapon with the same languor and stood staring at the dryad, eyes all over her lush body.

"Uh... hi," he said. "I'm Dominic."

"I am Kedra," she answered in a Slavic accent just as smooth as her verdant skin. "Welcome to my forest."

Kedra planted one hand on the curve of her hip, drawing every eye down to the soft green between her legs. I managed a sidelong glance and caught even Jun looking at the dryad. With an effort, I cleared my throat and stepped forward, inclining my head.

"I'm Stefano Rossi," I introduced myself. "There are werewolves in Les Krovi and I've come hunting them."

Kedra shuddered and folded her arms over her bare breasts. Her lovely mouth turned down in a scowl.

"They are savage and evil beasts," the dryad said.

"I intend to find and remove them from your territory," I told her. "Let us pass and they won't trouble you again."

Kedra's frown turned into a brilliant smile. Her emerald green eyes glittered and the fairy spread her arms, spinning a swift circle that showed off every inch of her nude body.

"Let you pass?" Kedra asked. "I will, but you come into my forest with two men. I want one."

"Uh...?" Dominic spluttered. "For what?"

"For sex," I answered.

"Really?" Dominic asked, grinning. He raised his hand in the air like a schoolboy. "Yes! I totally volunteer!"

Dryads enjoyed taking men as lovers... human, fae, djinni or just about anyone else. But that was a game, a sport. Not a price. If all Kedra wanted was sex, she could have lured us into her domain and seduced either of us off into the trees for a night – or month – of passion. She was looking for something more complicated than a simple fuck.

Kedra winked at Dominic and leaned in close, but suddenly drew back with a hiss.

"No, not you," Kedra said. "You have been tainted by demons!"

Dominic blinked, looking confused. "I what?"

"You were cursed," I reminded him. "Twice."

"But you guys cured me!"

"There's enough residual demonic power left in your system to make wiping your memories impossible," I reminded him. "Or you wouldn't be here."

"Aw, man..." Dominic sighed.

"Besides, sex isn't all she wants."

"What else is she after, then?" Dominic asked.

"A child," Kedra purred.

I knew what she would demand, but that didn't stop my stomach from knotting up. Dryads were all female and couldn't propagate their line without males of other species. But that had to be extremely difficult out here in the remote Russian wilderness.

"So few mortal men enter Les Krovi," Kedra said. "It has been over a century since I last seeded. You will give me what I need, Stefano Rossi, or you will never leave my forest."

Jun let out a small gasp and Dominic's eyebrows shot up almost into his blond hair. He whistled.

"Dude, she wants to get pregnant?" Dominic asked. "That is some serious shit. You'd have a kid, Stefano. And I'm guessing that dryad visitation rights are pretty sketchy. Are you okay with this?"

"No," I said. "But the Bitch is out there. I have to catch her and free her pack."

"Better to create new life than to allow death to escape us," Jun agreed.

"Wait, you're siding with the dryad on this?" Dominic asked. "I thought you didn't trust fairies!"

"They are mischievous," Jun said with a slow nod. "But if I could pay her price myself, I would. It is our duty to do whatever we must to stop the Bitch."

"Then we have an agreement?" Kedra asked.

"Yes," I said.

Jun turned to the dryad and held up her hand. "On two conditions."

Kedra frowned, but nodded at the geomancer to continue.

"First, when you have finished with Stefano, you will send us to the border of your domain," Jun said.

That was a good idea. Dealing with Kedra and her demands was costing us time we couldn't spare, but if the dryad's territory was half the size I guessed, magically sending us to the far edge would be helpful in getting close to the Bitch again.

"Very well," Kedra agreed. "And your second desire?"

"I watch," said Jun.

That one took me by surprise. Kedra laughed in delight and clapped her hands. I suddenly couldn't seem to get enough air into my lungs.

"You want to watch me fuck your friend?" Kedra said. "Yes, I agree to these terms!"

"Uh... Jun?" Dominic asked. "What the hell?"

"As you say, I don't trust her," Jun said. "She is fae and may play tricks we don't have time for. You can surely feel her magic already."

Jun gestured around us with a sweep of her hand to the thick, honey-colored light of the forest. I remembered the assault of intoxicating memories and nodded.

"Good point," Dominic said. "Too bad we didn't pack any mockfoil."

"Mockfoil?" I asked.

"For that spell, the one that protects you from fairy glamour. So she can't mess with your head, man."

I didn't actually know that spell. The College had maintained good relations with the fae since the days of Merlin himself. In sixteen years of hunting, I had only taken a couple of fairy bounties – occasional goblin troublemakers or an ogre who developed a taste for human flesh. Not exactly the kind of creatures with the power to cloud my thoughts. It always seemed far more important to shave a few minutes off my teleportation time.

"Well, since we don't have the ingredients," said Dominic, "I'll watch, too."

I quickly shook my head. "No. The Bitch is still out there and I need someone to keep an eye on the dowsing pendulum in case the pack changes direction."

Dominic sighed. "Lookout. Right. Hey, Jun? Want to trade jobs?"

"Perhaps next time," she said.

Was that a smile on the geomancer's face? Jun turned slightly, hiding her expression. Dominic grumbled about never getting the fun jobs as he took my backpack, then settled down with the pendulum in one hand and his shotgun across his lap.

"Follow," Kedra instructed.

The dryad spun on her toes and led us deeper into the cedar grove. I followed the soft green bounce of her ass, Jun pacing silently beside me. As covertly as I could, I slipped my wallet out of my back pocket and removed one of the folded squares of parchment inside. The smell of ginseng and mistletoe joined the scents of wood and leaves. Jun caught my eye.

"What is that?" she asked quietly, gesturing to my hand.

I hesitated, feeling my cheeks burn, but what was the point? Jun was about to watch me fuck a dryad. Decorum was right out the door and halfway down the block by now.

"Passion charm," I admitted. "It enhances desire, performance and ah... volume. We can't afford for Kedra to be unsatisfied."

Now Jun was definitely smirking. "And you just happen to be carrying such a spell in your wallet? Several of them, I believe."

I coughed and almost tripped over a tree root. Jun was right... I never knew when Lilith might have called me up for her unique brand of interrogation and I didn't want to disappoint, so it paid to be prepared. I supposed it was just habit by now.

I did my best to ignore Jun's question and jogged to keep up with Kedra. The dryad had stopped in a small clearing around the base of a huge, majestic cedar. The great branches spreading out overhead were each a tree in their own right and must have shaded nearly a quarter acre. Lush green moss carpeted the ground at my feet.

Kedra bounded across the glade to her tree and laid her hands against the vast red-brown trunk. Was she speaking to it? Preparing the cedar for what was about to happen in the shadows of its massive branches? I wasn't sure, but my heartbeat pounded and my pulse throbbed along the length of my cock.

The dryad turned to face me and licked her lips. Jun tensed beside me.

"You are in a hurry to get what you want, and so am I," Kedra told me in a soft, sultry voice. "Are you ready to take me, Stefano Rossi?"

"Yes," I answered.

I tore the passion charm in half and almost doubled over as the magical aphrodisiac took effect. My head spun and my heart hammered like the rapid fire of a machine gun. I forgot all about the embarrassment of what I was doing, that Jun was watching or even that Dominic waited just a hundred yards away through the trees. Blood roared in my ears and my entire being burned with sudden and intense need.

Kedra gave me no time to recover. She was on me in an instant, unbuckling belts and holsters and tearing at my clothes. The dryad didn't seem familiar with a lot of what I was wearing, but I helped her strip it all away until she had me naked for her unabashed scrutiny.

Kedra laughed in pure delight and pounced on me again. Her hands were all over me, pale green against my darker skin. She traced the dusting of hair across my chest, then followed the line of it down and down... I groaned in helpless, overwhelming pleasure as her fingers wrapped around the straining heat of my cock.

I pulled Kedra into my arms. The fairy woman's body was perfectly smooth and smelled fragrantly of cedar wood. I slid my hand along her spine to grab the curve of her ass, holding her tight to me. Her breasts were so soft against my chest, the nipples stiff points of sensation on my skin. I nuzzled her dark red hair, deeply inhaling the dryad's scent.

Kedra slid her hand up the hard length of my dick, forcing a long groan from my lips. I bit at the side of her neck to muffle the sound and tasted sweet rainwater on her skin. Kedra moaned as she stroked my cock between us, pumping pleasure into my body. My lust burned through me like something molten and already threatening to erupt.

Over Kedra's shoulder, I saw Jun standing at the edge of the clearing. The geomancer stood tensed, feet planted and hands at her sides. Her brown eyes were wide, though. Jun's fingers opened and closed rhythmically, slowly squeezing nothing.

Kedra pulled me effortlessly down into the thick moss beneath her tree. It was as soft as any mattress and contoured perfectly to her body and mine. Dryad magic... Kedra had nearly absolute control of the earth and plants in her domain.

And over me. Gods, I was so hard. Kedra wanted my cock, my cum, and I wanted to... No, I *had* to give it all to her.

The dryad's jade-green legs parted for me, silky thighs brushing against my hips. Kedra's pussy was flushed a dark emerald color, blazing hot and desperately wet. She wrapped her legs around me, pulling me in. I had only a second to gasp at her strength, and then my cock was sinking into the velvety heat of her. My gasp turned into a deep, rumbling groan. Kedra's back arched as she drove me into her.

"Yes," she moaned against my chest. "Fuck me! Give me what I need!"

I sank myself deep into Kedra's pussy. Her wetness ran down my cock, along my balls and the dryad's pale thighs in slick streaks. My every nerve was on fire and I burned with need. I grabbed Kedra's round ass and hammered myself over and over into the welcoming tightness of her body. She raked her nails down my back and dug her heels into my flanks, moaning and urging me on. The sweet scent of her made my head spin.

Faster! Deeper!

Wetness ran along my fingers, hot and slippery. Kedra threw back her head, making her dark red hair fan out across the mossy ground and exposing her tender green throat. I kissed her neck and felt her pulse flutter against my lips.

"Les Krovi is so cold," Kedra whispered. "And I am so lonely here. But you have brought me fire..."

The dryad twined her fingers through my hair and then pushed my head lower, shoving me against the softness of her breasts. Yes... I sucked her peaked emerald nipples into my mouth, one after the other, and flicked my tongue eagerly over the tips. Kedra's cries grew louder.

"I'm cumming!" she screamed out.

I hooked Kedra's legs over my arms to thrust myself ever deeper into her. I forgot all about the cold, sweat running down my tensed back as I worked the dryad hard through her long orgasm. Kedra writhed on my dick, panting and moaning with desperate, urgent desire.

I felt Jun's eyes on me and looked up, my hair in sweaty tangles across my forehead. The geomancer still stood in her battle-ready stance, but her cheeks were flushed dark and her pupils were dilated. Jun licked her lower lip slowly as she watched me. My hips jerked involuntarily at the sudden thought of those lips working up and down my cock.

Thick, hot pleasure coursed through me. It was too much... I was drowning in sensation, utterly subsumed by ecstasy, too much even for my passion charm to account for. I tasted Kedra on every heaving breath as I drove my cock into her. The dryad had caught me in her magic and I didn't care if I ever escaped. It felt so good, so perfect here with her...

"Fuck me!" Kedra said. "Fuck me deep and hard and fill me with your seed!"

"Yes..." I groaned.

I pumped my hips desperately into Kedra, buried myself to the hilt in her pussy and did exactly what she asked. What she demanded. I let out a sound that was half growl and half groan as I filled Kedra. Her magic and mine gripped me. The passion charm can make things pretty messy – that's part of the purpose. But in tandem with Kedra's glamour, the ecstasy was a hurricane roaring through me and into the dryad. I gushed cum into her, flooding Kedra's body until it ran white along the cleft of her ass.

The fairy purred with pleasure and pulled me back down to her soft breasts. I lay panting in her arms, but my dick was still achingly hard. Kedra kissed my hair and her pussy squeezed, caressing me and making cream ooze from her overstuffed slit. She kissed her way along the beard-roughened line of my jaw.

"It's been so long," Kedra said, punctuating her words by tracing the tip of her tongue along my ear. "And so are you."

Her pussy gripped me again and I gasped, hands tightening convulsively on her soft ass. Kedra laughed musically. She rolled us easily across the yielding moss until she came to rest on top of me, straddling me with my cock still buried in her silky depths. She stroked my chest slowly. Hunting monsters isn't an easy job and forced me to spend a lot of time working out. It was nice to feel like someone appreciated it... Pecs don't just happen, you know.

"I can show you so much pleasure," Kedra purred. She bit my ear. "Are you a naughty man, Stefano Rossi? Do you want to fuck my ass?"

"Yes," I growled.

Somewhere in the back of my mind, I knew that wasn't the right answer, but everything else seemed so unimportant compared to the feeling of Kedra's fingers closing around the base of my slicked cock. She lifted her hips and nuzzled the head between her soft cheeks. Yes...

And then another hand grabbed my dick, this one smaller and darker than those of the dryad.

"That will *not* get you pregnant," said Jun.

She was kneeling beside us on the ground, reaching between Kedra's legs to seize my cock. Jun's fingers tangled with the dryad's and slipped over my flushed length. I groaned helplessly.

"You have enough of his cum now, don't you?" Jun asked.

Kedra pouted and rocked back and forth, caressing my dick with the curve of her ass. Jun's grip tightened around me and my pulse pounded like drums in my ears. White beaded up on the darkened head of my cock and ran down over Jun's fingers, leaving a pale line all across them as though the geomancer wore rings of pearl.

"You said you would pay my price," Kedra said, leaning in close to Jun. "Perhaps you are jealous? You desire this man, too. You may join us, if you wish..."

Sinuous green shapes rose up from the moss around us, long and smooth. Each of the half-dozen vines terminated in a blunt, hooded cock. They swayed toward Jun, but the geomancer ignored them. Either dryad glamours were stronger against men or Jun's will was as firm as her grip. On top of me, Kedra tried to sink her pale ass down onto my dick, but Jun slid her hand up to the crown and into the fairy's way.

Two women fighting over my hard cock, stroking me and trying to stuff me into Kedra's eager little asshole... It was too much. My entire nervous system was on a magical hair-trigger. Jun felt the heat surging through my cock and pushed her other hand against the small of Kedra's back. The dryad gasped in surprise and then whimpered in pleasure as Jun fed the head of my dick into her dripping pussy again.

My fingers dug furrows in the soft loam at the sight of Jun and Kedra's hands working together now over my cock. With a loud groan, I shot a second huge load into the waiting fairy, filling and then overfilling her pussy until it ran in slippery white rivers down her thighs.

Kedra sat back, eyes shut for a moment, and then leaned in close to me. She trailed her green fingers along my heaving chest, up through my beard and cupped my cheek. The dryad gave me a long, slow kiss.

"I think he has paid your price," Jun said.

Kedra stood, finally releasing me. She stretched her arms up toward the spreading branches of her great cedar tree and smiled down at me as Jun grabbed my shoulder, pulling me into a sitting position.

"You have paid," Kedra agreed. "But you do not have to leave, Stefano Rossi. Let this woman and the other man hunt the monsters. You can stay here with me. Be happy and safe and loved every night here in my forest."

A hot shiver slid down my spine. I wanted nothing more than to say *yes*, to throw myself into Kedra's arms again and fuck her every day, in every way. My cock throbbed and another drop of thick white semen splashed into the carpet of moss. Jun's fingers tightened on my shoulder.

"Stefano," she said. "The Bitch."

I heaved myself to my feet, swaying and dizzy, but now my blood pounded out a different tempo entirely. The Bitch. The magic of the passion charm still coursed through me, pouring gasoline on the fires of my lust, but feeding every other passion, too – including the one to do my job.

A pack of werewolves was prowling through Les Krovi toward... something. I *had* to catch them.

"I can't stay," I said in a thick voice. "I... I have to go."

Kedra gave me another kiss that threatened to make my knees buckle, but broke off when Jun cleared her throat. Kedra laughed brightly and darted in to place a kiss on Jun's lips, too. The geomancer blinked a few times.

"Go, then," Kedra said. "You will find your way swiftly to the edge of my wood. Much faster than the werewolves did."

I picked my clothes up from the forest floor and struggled to redress. My cock remained as hard as any tree branch and was difficult to maneuver back into my pants. Jun supervised this process with the same attention she had paid to my mating with Kedra. Something about that was strange, but I was too drunk on magic to figure it out just then. The geomancer handed me my belts and shoulder holster, then used her steadier hands to buckle them all in place.

My clothes and weapons seemed to weigh hundreds of pounds. I ached to sink back down to the ground and let Kedra tear them off again. But there were werewolves out there. Somewhere. Jun pulled my arm around her shoulder.

"Kedra?" I asked, forcing my head up. "My daughter... will she have a good life?"

"Yes," said the dryad. "I will love our daughter and protect her. I promise."

I nodded and Jun helped me stagger away.

Chapter

TEN

The forest was colder outside the cedar grove and I had to pull my coat back on. The cool air helped me shake off Kedra's magic, though, and after a few minutes, I could walk again without Jun's assistance. But the young geomancer hovered at my side until we found Dominic waiting beneath an aspen tree. He jumped to his feet, worry all over his face.

"Stefano? Are you okay, man?" Dominic asked. "You were gone for hours!"

Hours? I shook my head to clear away the last of the mental fog and peered up through the trees. Dominic was right. The sun had been high in the eastern sky when Kedra led me to her glade, but now it hung low in the west.

"I'm fine," I told Dominic.

He didn't look convinced. "What happened? I was about ready to come after you. Did we get the dryad's uh... cooperation?"

"It's all taken care of," I said.

Dominic relaxed visibly. "So what was it like? Come on, give me details!"

"We have a job to do," I said. My blood was still burning a little too hot, though.

Dominic sighed and went back to the aspen tree to unplug his cell phone from a larger gray rectangle of plastic on the ground. A solar panel, I realized as he folded it up and stowed it in his backpack, to recharge his phone.

I shouldered my pack, too, and took the pendulum from the branch where Dominic had hung it. We could still get several hours of hiking in before the sun went down... and I didn't want to risk being anywhere near Kedra's domain when we stopped for the night. I wasn't entirely certain that I wouldn't go sleepwalking right back into the dryad's warm, welcoming embrace.

I gave the pendulum a swing and followed its bearing northeast, the other two falling in quickly behind me.

"So how did our fearless leader do?" Dominic whispered.

"Kedra is satisfied," Jun answered, also in a whisper. "Stefano was very... thorough."

"Sounds like I missed a good show."

Jun didn't answer that – not with words, at least – but Dominic laughed. I glanced back, but Jun wasn't scowling at him or breaking the boy into tiny pieces, so I let it go.

There was something stranger in Dominic's question than just interest in my sex life. I was neither fearless nor his leader, but he had called me *boss* several times now. I turned the problem over in my head and decided that there was only one logical conclusion: Dominic was an idiot.

We moved swiftly through Les Krovi. We weren't hiking any faster than usual, but within half an hour, we had left the cedars far behind. When we found a gap in the forest, I couldn't locate the dryad's tower-tall tree at all. I squinted down the hill we had just climbed. About two hundred seventy-five feet. Assuming a standard rural air quality and refraction index, that placed the horizon... twenty miles away. If I could no longer see Kedra's tree, then we had traveled at least that distance.

"How far have we come?" I asked Jun.

The geomancer swept her dark gaze across the forest, scrutinizing the landscape.

"About sixty kilometers," Jun said. "I think I can sense the nexus of Kedra's grove, but it is difficult to pinpoint this far away."

I nodded. Kedra had kept her word. With the same magic that could have had us wandering in circles for days, she had sent us to the edge of her domain. I checked my dowsing pendulum, noting the length of swing and tension in the chain. The bronze weight strained forward and seemed to hum, as though filled with bees. We were definitely closer.

"Let's keep moving," I said.

Jun and Dominic followed me without complaint through the afternoon. The ground cover in this part of Les Krovi was thicker, bushes and scrubby taiga grasses concealing stones and thick roots. But we also discovered fresh signs of the Bitch and her pack.

Dominic was the first one to hear the rough calls of the rooks. A stand of young rowan trees had been smashed to the cold earth and shattered into splinters. A dozen surrounding firs and pines were broken or gouged so badly that they would likely never recover. The dark bulk of a bear lay half-shadowed under the trees, gutted and still. Black birds reluctantly took flight as we approached, but they settled again nearby, waiting to return to their meal.

"Werewolves, right?" Dominic asked, holding his hand up to some of the claw marks and comparing their spacing.

I nodded. "Hunting or raging. Perhaps both."

Jun waved off a few black birds. They had gathered around a churned-up patch of earth and the geomancer knelt, inspecting the torn ground.

"What is it?" I asked.

"Rooks are not carrion birds. They did not come for the bear," Jun said. She pinched something up out of the dirt – an earthworm. "Cold ground like this is difficult hunting, though. It's hard to dig and the worms hide deep."

But not if werewolves tore up the half-frozen forest floor for them. Jun held the squirming worm between her fingers for a moment before setting it back down. It swiftly wriggled once more down into the dark soil.

"The Bitch has been gone long enough for birds to decide its safe and come hunting," I said. "But not long enough for the worms to retreat from the cold."

Jun nodded. "The pack was here today."

She straightened and dusted off her hands. Dominic finished taking pictures of the destruction and picked his way back through the shattered trees toward us. He held up one finger to me. It was sticky with sap.

"Some of the trees are still bleeding," Dominic reported. "Uh... sapping, I guess. But isn't sapping when you smack someone in the head and knock them out? Anyway, this damage looks pretty fresh."

"We're getting close," I agreed.

"What now?" he asked.

"We press on while we've got the light," I said. "Then we'll stop for a few hours of rest and figure out our next move."

Jun and Dominic nodded. We took one last look around the carnage and then hiked on, following the pendulum. Behind us, the squawking squabble of birds resumed.

We hiked until the sun set behind the forest. Jun was as light-footed as ever, but Dominic was soon stumbling over hidden stones and I called a halt. Dominic sagged gratefully against a pine tree and I held out a canteen to him.

"Stop here?" he panted.

"Not yet," Jun answered. "There is a ley line ahead that I need to access."

"How much further?" Dominic asked. "Like, how many toes will I break by the time we get there?"

"About a kilometer," said Jun.

"So three toes, then."

Dominic took a drink and tossed the canteen back. I caught it and checked the cap.

"Grab a flashlight," I told Dominic.

"Won't the Bitch see that?"

"The light shouldn't carry far if you keep the beam low," I said. "But if you fall and cut yourself, the blood scent will carry for miles on this wind."

"Good point."

Dominic dug through his backpack until he found a slender LED flashlight. He directed it down at his hand before turning it on, then squinted at the light and twisted a ring around one end to narrow the beam. When Dominic was satisfied with the level of illumination, he gave me a thumbs-up and we resumed hiking.

Now Jun took the lead, pulling us off the pendulum's course and following the winding silver line of a rocky stream. Even with his flashlight, Dominic struggled for footing and nearly fell into the water several times. After one splashing near miss, he spluttered at me.

"How are you not tripping all over the place?" Dominic asked.

"Practice," I answered. "I've been a hunter for sixteen years. On my first hunt, I almost fell off a cliff. Twice."

Dominic laughed. "Yeah? So how many hunts until I qualify for the fucking hot fairies job?"

"Ten," I said. "But werewolves count double."

Dominic jerked to a stop, giving me a surprised look. Okay, so I'm not as funny as Lilith, but he couldn't have been *that* shocked that I was trying.

"Stefano..." Dominic said. "You know this is the last one, right?"

"The last what?" I asked.

"The last werewolf hunt, dude. This pack we're after... they're the only ones left. When we catch the Bitch, it's all over."

I tripped on a stone. Dominic grabbed for my arm, but I recovered my balance and he backed off. Jun glanced over her shoulder for a moment, watching me. When I straightened and kept moving, so did the geomancer.

The last werewolves. Dorian and Sylvia said the Bitch was now responsible for all active lycanthropy curses – her pack. Dominic was right. If we cured them, there would be no more wolves to spread their curse. And with the wrath demons who created them locked away in the Nether, there would be no new werewolves.

My job would be done.

That thought was nearly enough to make me stumble again, but I managed to keep following Jun through the deepening night. No more werewolves, no more hunting them across forests and jungles and snowfields for days or weeks. The monsters I had become a wizard to defeat would finally be gone.

"Stefano?" Dominic asked. "You okay, man?"

I nodded, not trusting myself to speak just yet. I wasn't sure if Dominic could see my gesture in the darkness, but he didn't ask a second time. We walked in silence for another ten minutes before Jun signaled a stop at the base of a pine-covered hill.

"Here," she said.

Dominic pulled off his backpack and shined his flashlight in a tight circle. "We're nice and close to the stream. Good, I need to refill the canteens."

There wasn't much of a clearing, but I didn't want to risk a fire this near the Bitch, anyway. The trees around us grew straight and tall, with evenly spaced branches – the guiding effect of the ley line Jun sensed but I could not see. I hung the pendulum from one of the limbs and noted the forceful swing northeast.

"We're a lot closer now," I said. "So I'm going to ward the camp tonight."

"Right." Dominic unzipped his backpack and consulted his cell phone. "Chalk... silver fulminate..."

"Careful with that. It's extremely volatile," I cautioned.

"I know. I'll watch it," Dominic said.

He held the flashlight in his teeth and produced the warding reagents while I measured out a twelve-yard diameter. We poured the chalk and silver fulminate carefully into seawater collected at high tide. I stirred the mixture clockwise with a glass rod until the glass turned a smoky gray color, then exchanged it for a brush made of fresh anise.

"The ward will keep out any creature not native to this plane," I told Jun. "As long as it holds. Will that be a problem for you?"

The geomancer considered for a moment, then shook her head. "I don't think so. The ley line is magic of the Earth and should not be affected."

I painted the chalk mixture in a circle, chanting the spell to activate it, stopping at thirty-eight-inch intervals to draw sigils into the air with my fingers. When I closed the circle, the entire thing flared with silvery light and then went dark again.

"You should both be able to pass through the circle to get to the water or latrine," I told my two companions. "Dominic, you may feel a little discomfort."

"Because of the residual demonic energy?" he asked me, then sighed and gave a rueful smirk. "I'm never going to live that down, am I?"

"It also protects your memories and makes you resistant to all sorts of charms," I pointed out.

"But not immune," said Dominic. "I mean, I got pretty woozy around Kedra."

"Not as badly as Stefano," Jun assured him.

Dominic smirked and winked at me, then took a collapsible shovel from his backpack. "I'll go dig that latrine. Extra deep?"

"Yes," I said. "I'm not ready to let the Bitch know we're nipping at her heels just yet."

"You got it, boss."

I really wished he would stop calling me that. Dominic picked up his flashlight, kept it pointed downward, and crept off into the forest to begin digging. Jun walked a slow circle, inspecting the ward I had created.

"How long will it hold against werewolves?" she asked.

"That depends upon the werewolf," I answered. "Against five of them, if the Bitch decides to backtrack... Maybe a few minutes. There are stronger and more comprehensive wards, but they have to be built into a room or structure. This is the best I can cast in the field."

"May I?" Jun asked.

I had no idea what she wanted, but I just shrugged and gestured for her to go ahead with whatever she had in mind.

Jun stepped into the center of the circle, pushed up her tattered black sleeves and took a deep breath. She began slowly, moving her arms in sweeping arcs and taking long, careful steps. The geomancer's form was every bit as intricate and precise a ritual as what I had just performed.

Gradually, Jun's motions drew in, her circles becoming tighter and tighter until she knelt and pressed both palms flat against the earth. The silver of her I-Ching tattoos glittered in the darkness and I felt something change in the air, a tingle like electricity. Jun remained down on one knee for a moment, concentrating, and then stood and brushed her hands clean.

"That was beautiful," I said. "What was it?"

"I've bent some of the ley line's energy around us to create an additional barrier," Jun answered.

"Will it stand up to a werewolf?"

"I have never tested it against one," she admitted.

Jun shivered and I pulled off my coat, holding it out. She hesitated, but then accepted it with a nod.

"Thank you," she said. "The chi I gathered last night is almost exhausted."

So that was how she kept warm throughout the long, cold Siberian day. Jun pulled my coat around her shoulders. It was far too large on her slender frame and hung nearly to the ground like robes. Jun held up her arms, hands hidden entirely inside my coat's sleeves.

"There aren't a lot of laundromats in the middle of Les Krovi," I said, feeling my cheeks go hot. "So... sorry."

"It smells like an herb shop."

"Sorry, occupational hazard."

Jun shook her head, long black braid swinging. "No, it's fine. Will you be warm enough until I can recover my strength from the ley line?"

"I'll be fine," I said, but the words came out a little shaky.

It wasn't exactly a lie, but I was already feeling the chill through my shirt, raising goosebumps all along my skin. Jun slid in closer, staring up at me. Faint starlight shone across her face, illuminating the dark blush in her cheeks, too.

"Perhaps we could share...?" Jun suggested in a soft voice.

There was a crash and swearing from a few yards away. "Fuck! Stefano, what the hell?"

I turned away from Jun to find Dominic sprawled on his ass in the pine needles and pinching the bridge of his nose. Jun gasped and hurried toward him.

"Bèn dàn!" she hissed. "So sorry... the barrier... I forgot."

The geomancer swept her hands in a complicated spiraling pattern. Dominic got back to his feet, but would not move until Jun assured him – repeatedly – that he wouldn't smash into her defenses again.

"Are you bleeding?" I asked when Dominic finally stepped over the chalk circle.

"No," he said. "My nose hurts, but no blood."

I nodded. No more scent trail than usual, then. I looked at Jun, who gave us a sheepish shrug.

"My barrier is less... forgiving... of his demonic taint," she explained. "But I have created an exception for you."

"It's okay," said Dominic. He sniffed a few times, then looked at me. "I saw a couple of deer out there. They were just kind of staring at me. Their eyes were all white. Some of Baba Yaga's?"

"Probably," I answered.

"We're still cool with her, right?"

I took the hellebore flower from one of my pockets and inspected it by the glow of Dominic's flashlight. The petals were still blood red.

"That means we have her blessing, right?" Dominic asked.

"I wouldn't exactly call it a blessing," I said. "Permission, perhaps. But yes."

Dominic let out a long breath. "Oh, good. You said the ward would hold off things not from Earth, but I didn't know if that applied to zombie deer."

I wasn't sure, either. Baba Yaga's sacrifices originated on our own plane of existence, but no one knew much about the source of her power. Was it terrestrial? Or did the great Russian witch draw her magic from the fairy realm? Maybe the spirit world? Probably not the Nether, or else Lilith's seal would have destroyed Baba Yaga.

I didn't see much point in worrying Dominic over the finer questions of metaphysiology, though. My ward would keep a unicorn from eating our toes while we slept, or hold a werewolf at bay for a few minutes. But if Baba Yaga decided to kill us, my spell was nowhere near strong enough to prevent her from doing exactly that. And I doubted Jun's ley line barrier would do much better.

Dominic set down his shovel beside our backpacks. "You two hungry?"

"Yes," Jun and I answered at the same time.

Dominic laughed and pulled on the bottom of his flashlight, sliding a metal sleeve down to transform it into a small lantern. By the LED glow, he began assembling sandwiches from our supplies. Jun and I sat a few feet away on the leaf-strewn earth.

"Just how close are we behind the Bitch?" Dominic asked. "How soon can we start doing the job we came here for?"

"Tomorrow," I said.

Dominic's eyes widened and he glanced up from the slice of bread in his hand. "Tomorrow? Holy shit."

"How do we begin?" Jun asked.

"Stefano is usually the bait," said Dominic. "He lures a werewolf into his teleportation circle, then finishes the spell and they vanish off to the Tower."

"Dangerous," said Jun.

Dominic nodded. "Yeah, especially with five of them. So what's the plan, Stefano?"

"We deal with the werewolves one at a time," I said. "I'd like to take out the Bitch first. Without her, I expect the pack to fall apart."

"Do you think we'll get that lucky?" Dominic asked.

"No," I answered. "I expect the pack to protect their leader. We'll need to attract just one, then lead it away from the others so I can teleport it to the Tower."

"I can probably shoot one. That worked pretty well in Louisiana," Dominic said.

"You nearly got yourself cursed for a third time," I argued.

"I just mean that I can get a werewolf's attention."

"The Bitch will try to keep her pack together," Jun said.

"I can use salt in my shotgun to make sure it hurts," Dominic suggested. "There isn't much I remember from being cursed, but I *do* remember a lot of anger and pain. And chasing the things that hurt me."

I suddenly felt a little guilty for how many times I shot Dominic while he was under the influence of the wrath demon's curse. And Lilith had run over Dominic in her car, then shoved him off a cliff and into the bay. Anger and pain, yes... but Dominic had walked away from both of us without a scar.

Werewolves are scary shit.

"I can get one of them to chase me, I bet. At least for a while," Dominic said.

"We don't have salt shells," I pointed out. "I never use a shotgun."

"No, but I do," Dominic said. "And we're carrying three and a half pounds of salt. It's the base for your teleportation spell. We have enough for twelve castings."

It paid to have extra. Components could get wet or contaminated, compromising the spell. At that point, count yourself lucky if it just fizzles out. Blowing up in your face is by far the more likely outcome.

"We can use half a pound of salt and have plenty left for teleporting the Bitch's entire pack," said Dominic. "Twice. A bunch of it is even still in crystals."

I required a wide variety of salts in various consistencies for my magic, so I often carried it in larger crystals or grains – known more commonly as rock salt – and refined it down later into the required texture.

"I can pack the shells," Dominic said.

"Have you done it before?" I asked.

"Not by flashlight, but yeah. Sylvia showed me how to make up specialty ammunition. She said it would be useful if I really wanted to help the hunters."

Sylvia wasn't wrong about that. Dominic watched me for a moment, but when I didn't object to his plan, he grinned and passed out finished salami sandwiches.

"What about the rest of the pack?" Jun asked. "They will tear both of you apart. Especially if you are casting a spell."

I took several large bites of sandwich and mentally ran through my list of spells for something to stop four other werewolves. A ward? No, it wasn't strong enough to survive a twelve-minute teleportation casting. Silver shots to their legs, maybe? That would certainly slow them down, but that was a lot of precision shooting against fast, maneuverable targets. And in the dense forest of Les Krovi, line of sight would be short.

Dominic had already stuffed his entire sandwich into his mouth and shrugged. "I gog noffing."

"We need something else to hold the pack's attention," Jun said between bites. "If Dominic can lure a werewolf out to you, I can keep the rest of them focused on me. In fact, I believe this will work best if I get the pack's attention first and begin the chase. Then Dominic can pick off the one in the rear."

Jun was talking about playing the world's deadliest game of tag – a game that she had already very nearly lost when we met.

"How does that end?" I asked. "One of them almost ran you down last time."

"Like you, I will prepare," said Jun. "Do you have paper?"

Dominic snorted. "He's a wizard. Do you want paper or parchment? Or vellum? There's a difference, apparently. We've got like eleven kinds of pens and pencils, too."

"Sixteen," I corrected absently.

"Paper will do," Jun said. "And a pencil."

Dominic dusted off his hands and found Jun a blank notebook. I nodded down to her chest. Jun blinked at me and looked uncertain. Did she think I was checking her out?

"Pencils are in the top right pocket," I said. She was still wearing my coat.

"Oh," Jun said. Did she sound a little disappointed?

Jun found the pocket I had indicated, though she had to sift through several kinds of charcoal and sticks of sealing wax before finding a pencil. She folded her legs into a lotus position, pushed up the sleeves of my coat and shut her eyes.

The geomancer took a few deep breaths and then began sketching, eyes still closed. I recognized a winding line first – the stream we had followed on our way to camp. Jun's map was as accurate as any satellite photo, but was criss-crossed with several straight lines.

"Roads?" Dominic whispered, pointing.

"Ley lines," I said.

Jun opened her eyes and tapped one of the lines with the point of her pencil. "This is the ley line we are on now. These are all of the others that it touches."

Dominic squinted around our tiny, dark camp. "I can't see anything."

"Neither can I," I said. "But most supernatural creatures can see or at least sense ley lines."

"It's only my quicksilver tattoos that let me link my own meridians into the natural network," Jun said. "So I can read and use the lines."

Dominic finished packing our food away in plastic containers, then collected salt and boxes of shotgun shells. Using a pair of pliers, he pried open the red plastic casing and poured out the lead shot. I looked over Jun's map, inspecting her meticulous work.

"Knowing the terrain is always helpful," I said. "But werewolves run faster than we do."

"Faster than you, perhaps," Jun countered. "I can draw enough chi from this ley line to match a werewolf's speed."

The young geomancer had managed to keep just ahead of a lycanthrope for more than a day when she found us. I spent at least twenty hours a week at the gym, but I couldn't have done it.

Jun leaned in close, brushing back an inky strand of hair that had come loose from her braid. She wrote something on her map – I recognized the character for *air* – next to one of the ley lines.

"This one runs through the sky," Jun said. "I will follow it, and the pack will track me from the ground."

"Follow it?" Dominic asked. "You mean fly?"

"I mean that I can travel along the ley line's path, but... yes."

Dominic whistled softly. "Damn, girl."

"I believe that I can entice the pack into a chase," Jun said, blushing a little. "But probably not for long. I doubt the Bitch will let them hunt me for an entire day again. How much time does your spell require?"

"Only twelve minutes!" Dominic announced.

Clearly, my accomplishment was less profound than being able to run through the sky because Jun just stared blankly at Dominic. I pinched the bridge of my nose and sighed.

"See, it takes most wizards fourteen minutes to go through the teleportation inscription and incantation," Dominic said. "But Stefano's managed to–"

"Jun," I interrupted. "Are you sure you can keep the pack focused on you long enough for Dominic to distract one and for me to teleport it? And then get away afterward?"

The young geomancer sat silently for a moment. She had escaped a werewolf just a day ago, and then only barely. If the Bitch hadn't called her stray back to the pack, Jun would be dead. And so would I. That encounter was still hauntingly close – I could see the fear there in Jun's eyes. And I watched her push it down.

"Yes," Jun said. "I will do my part."

I nodded. "Then that's the plan."

"Rinse and repeat for the rest of the pack?" Dominic asked.

"Yes. We'll pick them off one at a time," I said. "Make as many of those shells as you can without taking us below six pounds of salt. I'll prepare the myrrh and blue vitriol suspensions."

Dominic flashed me a thumbs-up. "You got it, boss. I can measure out the salt for your teleportation while I'm at it."

"Good. Jun, how long do you need to channel the necessary chi from this ley line?"

"About four hours," she answered.

"And then everyone get some sleep," I said. "We need to be up and moving early tomorrow morning."

Dominic nodded. Jun shrugged off my coat and held it out.

"I will gather my strength from the ley line," she said. "Thank you for letting me borrow it."

I accepted my coat and pulled it back around my shoulders. Jun was right – the fabric carried a lot of my own strongly herbal smell. Any time not at the gym or on a hunt was spent preparing spells in my sanctum. But now I smelled Jun as well, her scent mingled with mine into something that made my heart beat fast.

"I owe you some thanks," I admitted.

"For what?" Jun asked.

"Without your... intervention, I would still be in Kedra's grove."

"Enjoying yourself very much," Jun said. "But I believe that your gratitude is sincere. You seem a man more driven by purpose than by desire."

She brushed one hand along my sleeve. A tiny smile flitted across the geomancer's face so swiftly that I wasn't entirely sure that I hadn't imagined it. Dominic glanced up from his lap full of salt and shotgun shells.

"Hey, Stefano," he said. "Have you thought about what you're going to do once this job is done? I mean, hunting werewolves has always been your thing. What happens when they're gone?"

I had no idea, but now wasn't the time to worry about it. I went to my backpack and began pulling out the reagents for tomorrow's teleportation spell. We all had preparations to make.

"Let's not get ahead of ourselves," I said. "We haven't caught the Bitch yet."

Chapter ELEVEN

*L*es Krovi was still dark and quiet when I woke the other two. I had spent the last couple of hours on watch. Even within the protection of my ward and Jun's ley line barrier, we didn't dare all sleep at once. Dominic grumbled inside his tent and the display of his phone illuminated rumpled blond hair.

"An hour before even my ass-crack of dawn alarm," he mumbled, squinting through his tousled hair at the screen. "Ugh. Next time, I want to hunt vampires. No early mornings."

"You volunteered for this," I reminded him.

Dominic groaned, but crawled out from his tent without any further prodding. I went to the flap of my own tent and whistled quietly. Inside, Jun sat up and stretched.

"Is it time to leave?" she asked.

"Yes."

Jun nodded and slipped out of my sleeping bag. After her meditation the night before, the geomancer had only slept for a few hours, but even that appeared to be optional. She seemed to have nearly boundless energy. Useful.

Dominic lit a canned alcohol burner to brew up some instant coffee. He downed one cup in a pair of loud gulps and sighed.

"Dude, my old boss would skin me for making coffee that bad," Dominic said. He thrust another lukewarm cup into my hands. "Good thing I'm not a barista anymore. Here."

I raised an eyebrow. "Didn't you just say it tastes awful?"

"Sure did," Dominic answered cheerfully. "But it's not even dawn yet and that shit is loaded with caffeine."

"You think I'll fall asleep on the job?" I asked.

"Not risking it. Jun and I are only bait. You're the one doing the real work, boss."

Dominic tossed me a protein bar to go with the shitty coffee and then began packing up camp. I offered the cup and plastic-wrapped bar to Jun, but she shook her head.

"Thank you, but no," she said. "I heard Dominic. I will sustain myself on the power of the ley line today, I think."

Jun turned away with a smirk and went to help Dominic. I finished my breakfast as quickly as possible and examined the demonic dowsing pendulum. It was barely swinging now, tugging only lightly out to the east. It required fresh ashes and crystal to be effective.

"Jun?" I asked.

The geomancer looked up from collapsing the tents. "Yes?"

"Are we close enough behind the Bitch's pack for you to sense them yet?"

Jun reached out with one hand to close her fingers around the invisible threads of the nearby ley line. She nodded.

"I can feel them. The pack is together and moving east."

If Jun could track the Bitch, there was no need to waste vampire ashes. They were difficult to acquire and would only become more rare as Lilith's seal prevented demons from creating more vampires. I found the box of grave dirt and put the pendulum away, trusting in Jun's magic.

I loaded my belt with bags and canisters of pre-measured salt, myrrh, pearlash, wormwood, cinquefoil and blue vitriol – enough to teleport a single target off to the Tower. The ground of Les Krovi was less problematic than the Louisiana bayou, but pine needles didn't make a very good surface for inscribing intricate spell circles. I made sure that the ebony charcoal was where it was supposed to be in the breast pocket of my coat, then inspected the sky. The sun hadn't risen yet, but I could make out a few slender threads of cloud eclipsing the stars. It didn't look like rain, though, and the ground was still dry.

I selected a rolled-up canvas tarpaulin from the bottom of my backpack. I had waterproof options, too, but the charcoal didn't stick as well to the waxed surfaces. Plain canvas with a tight, uniform weave worked best. I slid the bundled tarp under a strap for easy access and shouldered the pack. It was time to go catch a werewolf.

"Would anyone think less of me if I admit that I'm completely freaked out?" Dominic asked.

"I would think you insane if you weren't," Jun said.

"I'm not so sure that coffee was a good idea. I'm super jittery now."

"Beneath their curse, all werewolves are only human," I said. "Just like you were, Dominic. These people need our help. They don't deserve what the Bitch has done to them. We're going to help them."

Dominic let out a loud whoop, then clapped one hand over his mouth. "Sorry, Stefano. Just scared and excited. Let's do this shit!"

I turned to Jun, who was regarding me with an unreadable expression. Did she disapprove? But the geomancer had agreed to my rules on this hunt.

"Lead on," I said.

Jun nodded once and slid into motion, moving like a shadow through the darkness of Les Krovi. Dominic pointed at her shapely ass and nudged me with his elbow, but I grabbed his arm and hauled my assistant into the forest after her.

———

We traveled through the slowly lightening pre-dawn at a brisk trot, pacing ourselves but trying to close the gap. We passed more shattered trees, still bleeding amber sap, and even fresh paw prints pressed into the dark earth. I smelled blood on the air as we moved through the cold morning mist.

Not long after the sun began to rise, we heard the first distant howl. There was no mistaking that eerie sound for the call of ordinary wolves.

"Holy shit," Dominic whispered.

He was pale and a visible shudder worked its way along his lanky frame. But Dominic didn't break stride. He just hugged his shotgun tighter to his chest and clamped his lips shut. Jun's face had gone white, as well, but hardened as she guided us unerringly through the woods in the direction of the howls. We heard barks and yips now, too, then a single powerful voice silencing the others with a deep snarl.

Jun stopped midstep and Dominic almost ran right into her, but managed to jerk to a quiet halt beside the geomancer. All three of us hunkered down behind the trunk of a fallen tree.

The ground ahead dipped down into a shallow bowl. I could just make out a black silhouette stalking through the slanting rays of misty morning sunlight, too huge even to be one of Baba Yaga's servant bears. The Bitch was the largest werewolf I had ever seen – at least eleven feet tall, covered in sooty fur that silvered along her muscular chest and belly.

A smaller brown shape circled her, a young male growling low in his throat. There was a flash of the Bitch's demonic golden eyes, sharp claws, and then bright blood and pale bone as the other werewolf fell back, whimpering. The other three pulled away, ears and muzzles lowered in unwilling submission. The Bitch was disciplining her pack.

I barely dared breathe this close to them, much less whisper to my two companions. Instead, I pointed to the brown wolf, who was backing away from his leader with teeth bared and blood running down his flank. The wound to his leg would make him slower than the rest of the pack – a perfect target for my spell. But werewolves healed demonically fast and our advantage wouldn't last long.

Dominic gestured to the injured werewolf, too, then himself and nodded his understanding. I turned toward Jun. Sweat beaded along her dark hairline despite the cold morning, but she pointed a few degrees west, in the direction of the ley line she had marked out the night before. The one that arced up into the sky and would hopefully keep Jun away from the werewolves' deadly claws and teeth while they chased her.

Jun held up two fingers to Dominic. She wanted a two-minute head start to secure the pack's attention before he tried to separate the injured one. Jun would have to watch her speed if Dominic was going to keep up, even at a distance. But he just nodded again.

Then Jun and Dominic both looked at me, waiting for my signal to go. I would have liked to start my spell now, before sending them off to confront the pack, but there were too many aromatic components and the incantation alone lasted nearly five minutes. There was no way the werewolves below would overlook what I was doing for that long.

They were drawing together into a circle. A female with pale fur growled and leapt on the wounded male, clamping her jaws down on the back of his neck. She bore him to the ground as he twisted in her grip, snarling and bleeding. But the Bitch bounded in and lashed out with one thickly muscled arm. The white werewolf flew back and smashed through a pair of saplings before crashing into the forest floor hard enough that I felt the impact from the top of the hill.

The Bitch stood over the brown male she had bloodied not even a full minute ago, her black hackles raised. What was she doing?

Securing mating privileges? These were werewolves, not earthly creatures, but lust was certainly one of the passions that drove and transformed them…

The smaller female was on her paws again, ears flat along her skull, but she didn't pounce again. We had to move now, before the Bitch got her pack moving. I raised my hand and brought it down.

Jun hissed out a breath and jumped to her feet. She leapt over the log and sprinted down the hill, right at the pack. The Bitch's head snapped up and she fixed her yellow-gold eyes on Jun. The geomancer's tattoos shone with a cold silver light even through her clothes and left a shining trail behind her as she ran. The Bitch whirled toward her and Jun darted to the side, slicing one hand through the air. An icy, furious wind suddenly tore across the forest, whipping up leaves and pine needles.

The Bitch howled in fury and the rest quickly echoed her other-worldly call. As one, the werewolves took off at a dead run. The wounded male was the slowest, falling swiftly into the rear of the pack as they scrambled after Jun. She sprinted away through the trees in the direction of the aerial ley line.

"Holy shit," Dominic whispered again.

I began counting. Jun wanted a two-minute head start, so that was exactly what we would give her. I yanked the bundle of canvas from my backpack and Dominic helped me spread it across the ground. When that was done, I grabbed the ebony charcoal from my pocket and pointed west. The sounds of vicious howls rang all too loudly through Les Krovi.

"It's time," I said. "Go!"

Dominic unslung his backpack, dropped it behind the fallen tree that had been our cover, and turned the safety off his shotgun.

"See you on the other side," he said.

Dominic jumped over the log and skidded down the slope, then stretched out his long legs and loped off west through the forest to bring me a werewolf.

Watching Dominic and Jun run toward the Bitch's pack was nerve-racking. But not being able to see them was worse. No one else has ever been the bait for my spells, not since I was just a teenage apprentice following Sylvia through the mountains. Would Dominic be fast enough to catch up? Would Jun be fast enough to get away? Would the Bitch kill them both?

There was no room for questions right now. Dominic and Jun were buying me time, potentially with their lives. Twelve minutes of it, to be precise.

I knelt in the center of the tarp and traced out a circle of burnt ebony. The earth wasn't quite flat, but I would make it work. Raido and ehwaz runes at three-inch intervals to enclose the four interlocking rings. Myrrh and cinquefoil went at the north and south points of the first and third circles, east on the second and southwest by seven degrees on the last one. I poured the smaller ring of salt inside the last circle that would keep me from being transported along with my target.

I was five minutes and forty-seven seconds into casting when I heard the crack of a shotgun and a savage howl of pain. Dominic had engaged the injured wolf. There were more distant howls – the rest of the pack chasing after Jun. I spared a single glance up and out across the sea of trees. Silver light flashed over the treetops. Was that Jun springing up along the ley line?

I had six minutes and thirteen seconds of work left. I grabbed a vial from my belt, tore out the stopper and tipped the contents into my hand. Wormwood at the spell's heart, where all the circles overlapped, recognized and accommodated for the power of a demonic target. I threw the empty container aside.

Five minutes and thirty-three seconds remaining.

I took the final vials from my pocket and gave them a sharp shake, breaking the delicate wax seal inside that separated pearlash and blue vitriol. The chemicals rushed together, suspended in mineral oil, and began to churn as though boiled in a crucible.

I poured the concoction out into the glyphs that directed my spell to send its target to the Tower. They burned into the canvas at my feet with silver-black smoke. The mixture's potency wouldn't last long.

Another gunshot boomed through the forest, followed by a howl much closer than before. I heard wood crack and snap, almost as loud as the answering rapport of Dominic's shotgun. That was three shots – two left until he had to reload.

I drew a deep breath of cold morning air and began the incantation. This was what turned herbs and chemicals into true magic, that commanded space to twist in on itself and join one place to another. Four minutes and forty-seven seconds left... Hey, it takes a little while to convince reality to bend to your will. So I chanted as quickly and smoothly as I could.

Footsteps pounded through the leaves toward me and I heard the harsh rasp of labored breathing. Dominic burst from the trees and into the shallow bowl of earth below, running as fast as his long legs would carry him. His shirt was drenched with sweat despite the Russian cold and his chest heaved like bellows. Dominic spun on one heel, pumped his shotgun and fired out behind him, then kept running.

The small brown werewolf bounded after him. And by *small*, I mean only seven feet tall and three hundred pounds of muscle, claws and rage. There was no sign at all of the Bitch's wound as the werewolf tore through the woods after Dominic, faster than any human could run. But with twice as much mass, the monster's inertia made it difficult to change direction as Dominic darted his way between the trees. Frustrated, the demon wolf simply smashed a tall alder out of its way.

Dominic circled wide around the forest clearing. I had nearly two minutes left on my incantation – he knew I needed more time. But we've talked about werewolves and their instinctual hatred of Merlinic magic.

The beast skidded to a stop at the bottom of the hill, claws tearing deep furrows into the earth. Its long head whipped toward me and the werewolf howled, eyes burning with rage.

"Hey, fuck-wad!" Dominic shouted. "Over here!"

He fired his last shot into the werewolf's haunches. The salt didn't do much damage – especially through a lycanthrope's thick hide – but it stung. Dominic cheered as the wolf whirled toward the source of its pain, then he swore and began running again.

Forty-eight more seconds. I fought to keep my voice steady and the incantation even as Dominic fumbled in his pockets for more shotgun shells. A red cylinder of plastic slipped through his fingers. Reloading at a dead run was just about impossible and if Dominic slowed down at all, the werewolf would be on him.

He wasn't going to make it.

I kept chanting as I drew the revolver from my side. I couldn't step outside the ring of salt until the spell was completed. The circle of white was already darkening to the same color as the charcoal, struggling to isolate me from the seething power of twisting space. My magic was active, but not finished.

I sighted down the barrel of my gun. It was loaded with silver – not liquid silver nitrate, but a solid sterling slug for pure stopping power. The werewolf was moving too fast, and I had to split my attention between the shot and the spell. There was no way I could hit my target in the leg, so I aimed for the body.

Thirty-one seconds.

I pulled the trigger and the werewolf staggered. I fired twice more, slamming another pair of pure silver bullets into its ribs. The monster turned to face me again, snarling in pain and fury.

I had its attention now. The silver slugs would slow the werewolf down a little. Maybe not enough. If the teleportation spell wasn't done by the time the beast reached me, I was a dead man.

Twenty seconds left. The werewolf scrambled up the slope toward me, tearing huge chunks from the ground with each swipe of its long claws. It bounded over the fallen pine tree and kicked shards of rotting wood out in every direction. I swiped one out of the air before it could hit and disrupt my incantation. Just eleven seconds left to finish the spell, but the werewolf was almost on top of me.

Dominic charged in from the side, pumping the action on his reloaded shotgun. He raised it, fired and blew a cloud of red from one of the werewolf's knees. That shot wasn't salt and the monster sagged, blood running along its wounded leg. Dominic threw himself into the beast and tried to force it back a step. With only half the lycanthrope's mass, though, he bounced off and slid away down the hill.

The werewolf fixed searing yellow eyes on me again. Its lips peeled back from long white fangs in a lupine grin. Blood had already stopped flowing down its leg – supernatural healing worked quickly – and the werewolf pounced.

Too late.

I finished the incantation as it leapt toward me. Leaves and pine needles levitated up off the forest floor around us. The werewolf hung above me for a split second, and then vanished. A whoosh of air rushed into the sudden vacuum left behind and everything fell to the ground again.

Dominic's head popped up over the shattered log, dripping with sweat, but grinning hugely. "Dude! It worked!"

"Ssh," I hissed. "Listen…!"

The Bitch's voice rose up from Les Krovi in a long, mournful howl. I had never heard a werewolf make a sound quite like it and my blood ran cold. When the echoes fell away, the woods were silent.

After about ten minutes of tense waiting, Jun finally bounded down out of the trees behind us. Dominic gasped and brought up his gun. I shouted and raised my hand, but he stopped when he saw the geomancer.

"They are heading east again," Jun reported, panting to catch her breath. "The rest of the pack was chasing me, as expected. But when you completed your spell, the Bitch called them off. She knows what you did, I believe."

"We still don't know what she's after out there," said Dominic.

"No, but now she's got a smaller pack for whatever it might be," I said. "And the College can begin removing that man's curse on the next new moon."

Dominic smirked and elbowed Jun lightly. They both looked tired, but pleased.

"Our hunting methods don't seem so dumb now, do they?" he asked.

The geomancer smiled. "No. I admit that I'm quite impressed. What comes next?"

"One down, four to go," I answered. "Fifteen minutes to rest and clean up, then we tail the Bitch until we get close enough to do it all over again."

Chapter TWELVE

We hiked throughout the rest of the morning, staying close enough on the Bitch's tail that Jun could tell us which way to go. The pack turned north again as the sun had begun falling toward the trees and shadows swallowed the forest. Even Jun was slowing down when I finally called a halt.

"Thank god," Dominic panted.

He was in excellent physical condition, but the lean surfer was jogging with one hand pressed to his side. He sagged against a tree to wheeze and dropped his backpack on the ground.

"I'm starving," Dominic said. "Can I make a fire to cook us up some food?"

I considered for a moment. The Bitch was ahead of us and traveling fast. What were the chances that she would double back to check out the smoke? Not high, but I shook my head.

"Best not to risk it," I answered. "And I don't want to be here that long. We need to get moving again as quickly as possible."

"Okay," Dominic said. "I'll see what I can manage without a fire. We deserve more than protein bars after catching a werewolf!"

"You did well," I admitted.

Dominic threw his hands enthusiastically into the air, winced and settled for offering a fist-bump. Which I declined.

"I'll do better next time," Dominic said a little more soberly. "I'm thinking some silver nitrate to slow them down before I go in with the salt."

"We can't load liquid silver nitrate into a shotgun shell," I told him. "But I have some hollow-point thirty caliber bullets. Can you use a rifle?"

Dominic grinned, all gravity suddenly gone. "Hell yeah!"

"You'll still need the shotgun," I told him. "And managing two large guns at the same time takes a little practice. I can show you the trick to it when we stop tonight."

My assistant did a short, ridiculous happy dance before setting to work making a late lunch. I turned to Jun.

"Are we close enough to a ley line for you to recharge?" I asked.

"No. The closest one is a hundred meters out that way," Jun answered, pointing through the trees. "But I can go meditate there for a while to recover."

"I'll come with you," I said. "I'd like to get another map of what's ahead, if you can draw one."

Jun nodded and Dominic promised to have the food done by the time we came back. I told him to get the next batch of teleportation reagents ready to go, too.

"On it," Dominic said.

I tucked the notebook under my arm and followed Jun up a rocky scree slope. She leapt nimbly onto the top of a shattered granite boulder and crossed her legs beneath her. When the geomancer was situated, I handed her the notebook.

"The ley lines are thinning out to the northeast," Jun reported as she sketched. "If they don't intersect a stronger line soon, it will take me longer to draw on their chi."

"Are you in trouble yet?" I asked.

"No. I will be able to run and to fight. But there aren't enough ley lines in that area to track the Bitch," Jun said.

I nodded. Once we got closer, I would unpack and reload the dowsing pendulum. A deep frown crossed Jun's face, though, all out of proportion with the problem of tracking the werewolves. She drew swiftly across the page, filling in the map. I saw the sharp angles and altitude markings of steep mountains, and on the far side, something that wasn't more forest. It was a small grid of straight lines, but they didn't look anything like the other ley lines Jun had drawn.

Because they weren't ley lines, I realized.

Those were roads. There was a town beyond the mountains.

"Fuck me," I breathed.

Jun's eyes flew open, staring at me. I pointed down to the map.

"A town isn't good news," I said. "Can you tell how many people live there?"

"I can't feel individuals at this range," Jun answered. "But based on the size... about a thousand?"

"Shit."

Jun reached out hesitantly to touch my shoulder. "We may need to kill the pack to stop them."

"It won't come to that," I said.

"Four werewolves could turn that into a ghost town within hours. We may not have another choice."

I refused to look Jun in the eye. What she said made sense, but I couldn't bring myself to say so. Instead, I went back to studying the map. The town lay directly to the northeast, right in the Bitch's path.

Was that really a coincidence...? Most werewolves were rural hunters. Cities and towns were too crowded, too confusing for such wild creatures. It was one of the only reasons humanity had survived centuries plagued by lycanthropes. Werewolves in the wilderness were deadly enough, where they hunted down loggers and hikers with ease. But in the dense population of an urban center, a single wolf could slaughter hundreds before being caught. What would an entire pack do?

"How far away is this town?" I asked.

"At their current speed, a day and a half," Jun answered. "Maybe two. The mountains up ahead will slow them down."

"And us." I raked my fingers through my hair. It was still caught in tousled waves from the hunt this morning. I sighed. "Werewolves usually chase me, not the other way around. I've never had to compete with their speed like this."

"How many werewolves have you hunted?" Jun asked.

I didn't have to think about the answer. It was a number I knew better than my own age.

"Thirty-nine, including the one this morning."

"And you took them all alive?"

"No," I admitted. "Before I was a hunter or even a wizard at all, my father was killed by a werewolf and my mother was infected."

"You killed the werewolf that did it?" Jun asked.

"No, my teacher caught that one. But I killed my mother when she changed."

Jun slid her hand from my shoulder and down my arm. My muscles were bunched like knotted ropes and refused to relax, but even through my clothes, Jun's touch was enough to raise goosebumps. Her eyes were full of sorrow for my loss.

"I am sorry you had to do that," Jun said.

"But I didn't," I told her. "That's the point. There's a cure, Jun. I killed my mother because I was frightened and young and didn't know any better."

The geomancer's hand was still on mine, running her thumb over my knuckles. I wondered if she felt the scars there. Jun smiled at me.

"You are quite impressive," she said, then blushed. "I mean your work is impressive. You and Dominic make a good team."

"We're not a team," I said automatically. "He's just... tagging along."

Now one of Jun's eyebrows arched into a delicate black bow. "You called him your assistant before, when we were..."

She trailed off, but I remembered. When we laid together under her shield of earth, my cock hard and pressed against her stomach.

"There is power in numbers," Jun said. "One is auspicious."

"But two is better?" I asked.

"Three is better."

"You've been a great help," I confessed. "I know I put up a fight, but... thanks for coming along."

"I have not shown you all that I can do, but I would very much like to."

I wasn't sure how to interpret that. Was Jun flirting with me? An invitation to throw her down onto the ground and finish ripping those torn pants off her smooth, slender body?

I had no idea what Jun wanted. But I knew where the Bitch was going... And I knew I couldn't let her get there.

Jun drew back, regarding me uncertainly. Her high cheeks were flushed crimson and she had crumpled the map she had drawn in tightening fingers. Slowly, she brushed it flat against her thigh.

"We need to catch up," Jun said in an unsteady voice. "Or get ahead of the pack somehow."

I pointed to a curving trail of graphite across the page. It started a couple of miles away from us and then ran up into the mountains.

"What's this?" I asked.

Jun narrowed her eyes at the map, then closed them and tilted her head back, exposing the soft skin of her throat. She must have been feeling along the ley line for an answer to my question. After a moment, Jun opened her eyes again.

"A logging road, I think," she said.

"Traveling on a road would be a lot faster than winding our way through the forest. Can you tell if it's passable?"

"I am not sure," Jun said. "It runs through the dead zone, where the ley lines give out, so I can sense few details. But it goes roughly the right direction and may lend us an edge in speed."

I stood. "How long do you need to recover the chi you expended today?"

"About an hour."

"Do it," I said. "And then we resume the hunt."

Chapter
THIRTEEN

Dominic looked at Jun's map while we ate. Quickly. He shook his head in bewilderment.

"You really think the Bitch is taking her pack into a town?" Dominic asked. "I mean, she has enough trouble controlling them out here in the forest. With all the smells and distractions of a town, it's going to be nuts. Bloody, but nuts."

As he well knew. Dominic's lycanthropic rampage through the city had been chaotic, deadly but unfocused.

"That may be," I said. "But the Bitch exerts an unparalleled level of control over her pack. She stands a better chance of directing an urban slaughter than any other werewolf I've ever encountered."

"She stopped them from hunting me," Jun agreed. "Twice."

Dominic shuddered. "Fuck. So what's the plan? Teleport to that town and intercept the pack?"

"No. The Bitch still has her pack," I said. "If we intercept them too close to that town, we wouldn't have the time to catch each one individually. Even if we got lucky enough to snare the Bitch, that leaves three lycanthropes left to go rampaging through the human population."

"So we'd have to catch the entire pack all at once," Dominic said. "Yeah, I wouldn't want to roll those dice."

"But if we can thin out their numbers before they reach the town, then your teleportation idea isn't a bad one," I admitted.

Dominic grinned. "Okay, where's that logging road you found?"

"Here," Jun said, pointing. "It runs northeast, the same way that the Bitch went."

"Can we just teleport *there*?"

I considered that for a moment before shaking my head. "The quantity of circles and the amount of reagents used depends upon the number of targets. Trying to move three of us in short hops will eat through our supplies too quickly. Longer jumps and we might overshoot the pack. If we're lucky…"

"If we're not lucky?" Dominic asked.

"We could appear right in the middle of them."

"Damn," he sighed, but then perked up. "Looks like I'm getting more cardio today."

"We all are," I agreed. "Jun, do you have enough chi? We won't cross another ley line for a while."

The geomancer nodded. "I am ready."

"I've got the stuff for your next teleportation weighed out," Dominic said, pointing to a row of bags and canisters. "But if Jun won't have access to ley lines, that means she can't track the Bitch, right?"

"Right," I said.

"Then should we load the dowsing pendulum again?"

"Not yet," I answered. "We know where the pack is going and I don't want to waste our supplies or our time."

Dominic nodded and we quickly cleaned up lunch, then shouldered our heavy backpacks. Jun and I consulted her map. When we agreed on the shortest route to the logging road, I pocketed the map and we got moving.

———

It was late afternoon when we reached the logging road. The ancient tire tracks were wide and cut deep into the cold brown earth. Sundered stumps lined the road in ranks, but the saplings growing up between them were almost as big around as I was. The lumber trade in this part of the *blood forest* had apparently dried up many years before the Bitch's arrival.

Baba Yaga, perhaps? Had she taken some offense at this intrusion into her domain? Maybe. Jun confirmed that there were no ley lines in the area. Perhaps that was the result of the great Russian witch's wrath.

But it was equally likely that the cause here was simple economics – the town on the far side of the mountains was the closest center of civilization. That was a long way to haul wood, especially if there was a closer supply.

It was dark and cold in the shadow of the mountains, even with the descending sun still dappling the western forest in pale golden light. Night came early this far north. Despite the deep wheel-ruts, the logging road was fairly level and would have made a good place to set camp – a truck driving through didn't seem very likely. But we finally had an open stretch of ground and I wanted to make it work for us.

"Let's press on," I said. "If we're lucky, we might be as fast on the road as the Bitch is in the woods."

"And you don't have to stop and beat us into obedience every few miles," Dominic added with a smirk.

Jun laughed, then fell suddenly quiet. She staggered to a halt in the middle of the road, staring into the darkness of Les Krovi.

"Shénme?" Jun gasped.

"What is it?" I asked.

"Something is disturbing the feng shui of this place."

"But I thought there were no ley lines here," I said.

"There aren't," Jun agreed. She pressed her hands to her stomach. "But I can feel it in my own chi...!"

Les Krovi was silent. I couldn't hear a single bird or chittering squirrel. Not even the wind whispered through the forest... But something moved in the darkness out beyond the edge of the road, a shadow stalking between the sundered graves of ancient trees. A shadow with black fur and golden eyes.

The Bitch leapt up onto the shorn top of a stump and howled. The werewolf's yellow eyes flashed and her fang-filled mouth was pulled into a tight lupine grin. Hooked claws like knife blades bit into the wood beneath her paws.

Two more werewolves jumped out from the trees, loping on long legs between the broken stumps and toward the road. The final member of the pack bounded over the moss-covered hump of a rock on our other side. I drew my revolver and Dominic scrambled to do the same, ripping the shotgun off his backpack.

"Holy shit!" he shouted. "What the hell are they doing here? I thought they were miles ahead of us!"

"The Bitch laid a trap," I said.

"They can sense ley lines," Jun gasped. "She knew there are none for me to use here!"

"Can you get away without one?" I asked.

Jun whirled, trying to watch me and four werewolves all at once. "Just with the speed of my own chi? I... maybe..."

"Then get out of here!" I told her.

"No! I'm not leaving–" Jun hissed and then cut off as one of the werewolves lunged at her. The geomancer threw herself into an aerial leap and landed in a crouch behind the demon wolf.

I brought my gun up and snapped off a shot. The silver tore a red hole through the werewolf's white pelt and sprayed blood into the air. It snarled and spun toward me. Dominic dashed to the side, trying to flank the monster so that it couldn't face both of us. He fired, pumped his shotgun and then pulled the trigger again, ejecting empty shells into the road. But Dominic's gun was still loaded with salt and the stinging shots had absolutely no stopping power.

Jun darted in from behind, hammering a high kick into the pale werewolf's spine that sent it skidding back through the half-frozen dirt in utter defiance of the geomancer's tiny size. She had filled up her own chi reserves, Jun said, and they would make her powerful. For a while.

I put another silver bullet into the white wolf's knee, and then the other two had closed the distance between us. A smoke-colored male charged and Dominic shouted, firing a shell full of salt into its face. The werewolf drew back, snarling in fury, but swiftly shook off the pain and slashed at Dominic again with long claws. I fired two silver shots through its gray-furred shoulder and Dominic flung himself out of reach.

The third wolf leapt at me and I grabbed one of the pouches off my belt. I crushed the red wax seal in my hand and shouted the word to invoke the fireball spell. Flames erupted between my fingers and I hurled them at the werewolf. My spell hit it full in the chest, slamming the beast ten yards back along the road.

The Bitch raised her dark muzzle and let out another howl. I grabbed Dominic by the sleeve and yanked him away from the white werewolf, then threw myself down on top of him as the gray one tried to rip my head off. Long fangs closed on my collar, tearing through the sweat-soaked cloth. I felt hot breath against the back of my neck and I twisted, lashing out desperately. I punched at the snout questing for my spine and smashed right into the werewolf's sensitive nose. It howled and released me.

I jumped up and tried to pull Dominic with me, but another huge, furry shape hurled me back. Dominic shouted my name and rolled to his feet, pumping his shotgun, but it was empty. He swung it like a club at the third lycanthrope – a lanky young male with cinnamon fur – who just kicked the gun away. Dominic managed to keep ahold of his weapon, but the blow drove him back down to his knees.

The white werewolf had changed targets again, now snarling and snapping at Jun. She kept it at bay with punches and kicks – at least, I think that's what she was doing. The geomancer moved too fast to see, but if she slowed down for an instant, that werewolf was going to gut her.

Across the logging road, the gray werewolf was on its feet again. Its chest was still blasted into a black crater by my fireball, but even as I watched, the ruined ribcage snapped itself back into its natural shape – if any part of a werewolf could ever be called natural – and the beast shook out its sooty fur. The werewolf lowered its head and snarled at me, lips skinned back from a nightmare of sharp white fangs.

There was one more silver bullet in my revolver. Not enough stopping power there unless I put the shot right through the werewolf's eye, so I grabbed another fireball from my belt.

The Bitch had been watching her pack harry us, long red tongue lolling from her mouth, but now the queen of werewolves was done being a spectator. She yanked an entire pine sapling out of the earth and hurled it at me. The tree spun through the air, whipping the roots at the bottom in a heavy arc as deadly as the biggest medieval mace.

"Get down!" I shouted.

Dominic and Jun threw themselves to the ground. I broke the seal on my spell and flung it at the tree. I missed the hurtling target of the trunk, but the branches whistling through the air caught the expanding orb of flame. I dropped to my knees as the fireball exploded outward, blasting the sapling to flinders. Wooden shrapnel peppered the werewolves all around us, but it was little more than splinters to these monsters.

"Stefano!" Dominic cried. "What do we do?"

"Get to the trees!" I shouted.

Jun leapt to her feet and I grabbed Dominic by the arm. I heaved him upright and we ran toward the darkening woods. The Bitch loped after us, scattering smaller wolves out of her path with a roaring snarl. They fell in swiftly behind her and the whole pack gave chase.

We had to lose them in the forest. But werewolves were so much faster than humans. Their senses were better, too. After all of our efforts to get close to the Bitch's pack again, now we had to get away. But how?

We plowed through saplings and over stumps, sprinting toward the forest. I heard snarls and splintering wood behind us, but every second the werewolves had to spend ripping up trees was one less spent trying to tear our heads off.

I pushed Dominic ahead of me and managed to shove my revolver back into its holster, then grabbed the last fireball from my belt. It would just slow them down for a moment, and then only if I could hit them all. I grabbed a handful of dried cinquefoil from my pocket. It was measured out for the teleportation spell, but I sure wasn't going to get twelve minutes to cast that now.

The cinquefoil couldn't expand the radius of my fireball. That kind of spell modification can take years of calculation and careful experimentation. But maybe it would still help...

I flung the cinquefoil out behind me, back toward the quickly closing werewolves. Lycanthropes may hate Merlinic magic, but that doesn't mean they know much about it – the pack drew close together on one side, running around the heap of inert herbs. Before they could spread out again, I cracked the seal on the final fireball, aimed, and threw with a shout. My spell detonated in the middle of the pack in a flaming thunderclap, scattering the werewolves. The air filled with the acrid reek of burning fur and howls of rage.

The Bitch was the first back up on her feet. Half of her elongated face had been blasted down to white bone, but raw red skin stretched out across the wound, already bristling with black fur. Smoke billowed from her huge shoulders like an ethereal cape of darkness even as embers glowed balefully in her pelt.

Jun and Dominic were almost at the edge of the woods. But how much protection could the forest offer? We would never be able to outrun the werewolves. I was out of fireballs and couldn't cast a teleportation circle on the run, but there had to be some other spell that would distract the pack long enough for us to get away...

"Dominic!" I shouted. "I need valerian root, clove oil, cuprite and lye!"

"A Janus mixture?" he asked, panting.

"Yes!"

Dominic skidded to a stop beside a cracked and moss-covered stump. He dropped his shotgun and ripped off his pack. I snatched the canvas tarp from my back and threw it down, kicking it open across the ground. Dominic yanked the scales and the canister of valerian root from his backpack, muttering measurements and instructions to himself.

"We don't have time to measure," I told him.

Dominic stared at me with wide eyes. "Stefano, I can't–!"

"I need that Janus mixture now!" I barked.

I fell to my knees on the canvas, grabbing the ebony charcoal from my pocket. A hundred yards away, the Bitch seized one of the other werewolves by the scruff of the neck and heaved it back to swiftly regenerating paws. She drove the pack before her with snaps and swipes of her hooked claws.

"Jun," I said. "Cover us!"

Pale-faced and sweating, she nodded once and ran to meet the closing lycanthropes. Jun ducked the claws of the werewolf in front – moving so fast that her shining tattoos left blurred silver trails through the darkness – and launched a spinning kick that connected like a car crash. Another werewolf darted in from the side, forcing Jun away, and the one she had hit straightened, broken bones popping back into place with one sickening crunch after another.

I wrenched my gaze off of Jun fighting for her life – and ours. I gripped the ebony charcoal tight, leaving smudges of black across my white-knuckled fingers, and traced out the dagaz and ansuz runes. For spells like the dowsing pendulum, they were written upright to grant awareness and clarity. But on the canvas at my feet, I inverted the runes to reverse their effects.

The pack smelled my magic and the white werewolf darted in toward me. Jun drove it back with a series of open-handed strikes, then flipped acrobatically away from a vicious answering bite. Sweat plastered strands of black hair to Jun's face like lines of ink across paper. Even with her augmented chi, she was tiring quickly. And Jun wasn't like Lilith – I couldn't just fuck her to restore that lost energy.

The Bitch grabbed Jun out of the air and smashed her down into the ground. The geomancer hit hard enough to leave a shallow crater in the forest floor and I heard the sharp sound of cracking ribs. When she jumped back up and toward the Bitch again, there was a bright red line of blood running from the corner of Jun's mouth.

Dominic shouted in pain and I half rose to my feet. Smoke sizzled from the back of his hand where he had spilled the lye onto his wet, sweaty skin. Dominic snapped his mouth shut, screaming through clenched teeth as he stirred the mixture.

"Dominic?" I asked.

"I... got it," he bit out. "Almost done...!"

One last stir and the bronze bowl rang like a struck bell on top of the stump. Dominic snatched it up and thrust the completed Janus mixture into my hands. I opened my mouth to ask for the belladonna, but Dominic already had the leaves and held them out to me. He knew what spell I was casting.

"Reload that shotgun and go help Jun," I said.

Dominic scooped up his weapon and grabbed a handful of shells from his pocket. The red-brown werewolf closed on Jun in two leaping bounds and slashed out, coming back with shreds of her ruined shirt on its claws. Dominic jammed the shells home into his shotgun, cocked it and fired to give Jun some cover.

I dipped the belladonna into Dominic's hastily mixed Janus mixture. The leaves smoked and took on a glassy black sheen like obsidian. I placed them at the cardinal points of my charcoal runes and stood.

"What are you doing?" Jun cried.

I met the Bitch's gaze and raised my hands. How well did she still understand human speech?

"Summoning help," I said.

I began the incantation. This one was much shorter than the teleportation spell. After all, I wasn't trying to sweet-talk existence into tying itself in knots this time. But the forest around me rippled like the surface of disturbed water.

The Bitch roared in instinctual fury as my spell took hold. She smashed Dominic aside with a backhanded blow and he tumbled through the darkness, crashing into a pine tree. He groaned as he sat up and blood stained his blond hair red. Dominic ejected the final shell from his shotgun, but his hands were shaking as he struggled to reload.

Jun was a streak of starlight-silver as she hurled herself at the Bitch. The geomancer and the werewolf twisted and tangled together in a dance too fast and too intricate to follow. I traced shapes into the air, angles and lines and solid surfaces described by my fingers spread wide. Shadows and light swam through Les Krovi like demonic willow-o-wisps.

Dominic squinted through the blood sheeting down his face and managed to stuff a single shell into his shotgun. But the gray werewolf spotted Dominic and bounded toward where he had fallen. The boy gasped and jammed the breach shut on his gun, aimed and fired. Lead shot sprayed out and peppered the lycan-thrope's fur in black and red. It reeled, but then whirled on Dominic again. Powerful infernal healing forced the buckshot from its body like seeds being nightmarishly planted in reverse.

Jun was still fighting to keep the other three werewolves at bay. She leapt up into the branches of a rowan, but the Bitch felled the tree with a single blow of her massive paw, driving her prey to the ground once more. Jun staggered back, limping and holding one hand to her side.

Dominic pushed himself away from the gray werewolf, but his back was against the tree he had crashed into. The wolf snarled and prowled forward, flexing hooked claws. I needed more time to finish my spell than Dominic had. My partner stared back at the werewolf, amber eyes meeting hard, resolute green. Dominic knew he wasn't going to be cursed this time. He was going to die.

"Enjoy it, motherfucker," Dominic panted. "Because this is the last time you get to hurt anyone."

I drew my revolver. One shot left, one silver bullet.

I aimed and pulled the trigger. The werewolf's golden eye exploded in a red gout of blood. It jerked up and away from Dominic as my bullet punched into its brain. Fur and hundreds of pounds of demonic muscle vanished and a naked human man slumped to the ground.

Dead. The revolver tumbled from my numb fingers.

"No!"

Someone was screaming and I realized that it... it wasn't me. The voice growled like a poorly maintained engine, but there was no mistaking the word or the raw anguish in it. The Bitch cried out for her fallen packmate – in English.

She leapt over Jun, ignoring the geomancer, and charged at me. I fell to one knee, choking out the final words of the incantation, and slammed my left hand down onto the ansuz rune. Belladonna leaves shattered like broken mirrors all around me and the embers floating through the forest flared with light.

And then they went dark.

For a moment, everything in Les Krovi went still. Even the Bitch dug her claws into the earth and jerked to a halt, staring up into the gently swaying trees behind me. Wind whispered in the branches, secretive and soft.

An army of undead animals burst from the forest. Hundreds of rabbits, squirrels and deer bounded in unnatural silence through the night, followed by the larger beasts of the woods – bears and tigers, lynxes and a pair of leopards. A thousand white eyes stared straight ahead, dead and flat.

Something even bigger than the tigers emerged from the shadows. Baba Yaga's cottage stalked out of the forest and towered over us all on thirty-foot bird legs, eclipsing the stars and moon in utter darkness. The light of a single candle flickered in the window.

The Bitch scrambled back, staring up at the walking cottage with burning eyes. The other two werewolves ran this way and that, trying to pick targets out of the sea of dead animals. But there was no scent, no taste of blood when one of them caught a skeletal rabbit in its teeth – the pale-eyed animal simply melted away into mist. The Bitch shook her head in confusion and leapt after her pack as the great chicken-legged hut took a massive step toward them.

"Jun, get Dominic!" I shouted.

The geomancer staggered through ghostly waves of charging animals. None of them spared her even a glance, and Jun was quickly at Dominic's side. She put one arm under his shoulder and heaved the boy up to his feet.

"I'm okay," Dominic groaned. "Stefano!"

Colors burst and swam across my vision. I fell twice before I finally managed to stand and stumble through the chaos, kicking a wolf away into wisps of fog.

Jun and Dominic ran toward me, flinching back from the pale flood of silent animals. Dominic swiped blood out of his eyes with one sleeve and Jun gaped at the huge shape of Baba Yaga's cottage, chasing the retreating werewolves off down the road.

"The spell won't last for long," I said. "Go!"

We limped into the forest as fast as we could.

Chapter
FOURTEEN

I ran through Les Krovi, stumbling on roots and stones. Colors swam across my vision and dripped like paint over the world. Darkness bloomed around me, ink dropped into the well of colors. Someone or something burned in the distance. I staggered, caught myself on what felt like a tree, and kept running.

"What... what was that?" Jun asked. Her voice sounded far away, though the quicksilver gleam of her tattoos was close beside me. "How did you summon Baba Yaga?"

"Not real," I gasped. "Only an illusion."

The real Baba Yaga was just as likely to attack us as the Bitch if we pissed her off. And in any case, there was no spell to summon the great forest witch. But the werewolves didn't know that. Even when their claws and teeth closed on nothing, they still didn't understand that it was a trick.

Black shadows ebbed and flowed across my vision as though they breathed. I smelled gasoline and the sharp iron tang of blood. I saw a pickup truck wrapped around a tree, my mother pinned behind the steering wheel and blood gushing down her slit throat. Her dead white eyes fixed on me and her lips moved in a silent whisper.

I turned away from the vision with a choked cry and ran. A voice called my name. My mother...? No, she was dead. I killed her seventeen years ago.

I reeled and pressed my hands into my eyes. Someone grabbed my shoulder and I pulled back with a snarl. I had to get away. From what, I had no idea, but the panic and horror rose inside me like floodwaters. I was drowning.

"Stefano!" Dominic shouted. "What the hell is wrong with you?"

There was another hand in the center of my chest, smaller than Dominic's. I tried to shove past, but Jun stood in front of me, short and slender and as immovable as stone. She narrowed dark eyes at me.

"Your chi is in turmoil," Jun said. "It's tearing itself apart. What happened?"

"My spell," I answered in short gasps. The ground beneath me seethed like a nest of snakes. "We were rushed, unprepared and the illusion backfired. I'm... seeing things."

Jun's skin turned as green as Kedra's for a moment and she frowned.

"How do we fix it?" Dominic asked.

"We don't," I said. "The College or Castle could help, but they're too far away. If I'm lucky, it will pass."

"And if you are not lucky?" Jun asked.

"Then the hallucinations don't stop and I lose my mind."

I stepped around Jun and kept moving. Dominic grabbed my shoulder again. His hand was shaking. Or maybe it was me.

"Shit. Shit!" Dominic said. "Stefano, stop! We need to stop. You have to rest!"

I wanted to protest, but I couldn't remember how as Jun and Dominic pulled me through the forest. They took my backpack and then pushed me down to sit against a fallen tree. Light and color raced across the sky in waving, knotting lines. We were too far south to see the aurora. Oh, well... I didn't know the names of the colors slithering there between the stars, anyway. If they even had names.

"We have to get him back to the College," Dominic was saying, whispering urgently to Jun.

"How? Stefano is the only one who can cast the teleportation spell and there is no way he can do that right now."

"Fuck!" Dominic hissed.

I pressed my face into my hands and tried to breathe slowly, deeply. But there was something at my feet, something pale and naked and terribly still. A dead man, the gray werewolf I shot and killed.

I reached out, but my hand passed right through his face. He wasn't real. Not here, at least. The illusion or hallucination – I was no longer sure which it was anymore – dissolved into wisps of mist and vanished in the darkness. But back beside the logging road, a real man lay dead. There was no magic that could help him now.

Something hot dripped into my hands. I held up my fingers. Not blood, I noted with a detached sort of surprise, but tears. I was crying. A sob fought its way from my chest. I saw a wolf running through the forest, gray and ghostly as fog. It leapt up across the sky and disappeared into the moon.

"I killed him," I choked out. "I came here to save them, but I killed that man."

There was a clatter as Dominic dropped something.

"Fuck! This is my fault," he said. "I'm sorry, Stefano. I screwed up the Janus mixture, didn't I?"

My head fell back against the tree behind me. "Maybe. But I told you not to measure it out. And I didn't have time to check my lunar charts, either. The moon... it influences sensory spells..."

"Don't you dare let me off the fucking hook, Stefano!" Dominic's voice was rough. "I'm the one who got cornered by that werewolf. It's *my* fault you had to kill him! You were right – I was stupid to think I could ever help!"

"Shut up," Jun snapped. "You have helped him every day since I arrived, Dominic. But you're not helping now. Make camp as best you can."

"Right. Yeah, sorry. I... I'm on it." Dominic looked at me, worry naked on his face. "But what about Stefano?"

Jun turned toward me, too. She crouched and took my hand in hers. The geomancer's touch was warm, but I shivered. Two moons shone in the sky, one silver and the other as red as blood.

"I think I can help him," Jun said slowly.

"You can?" Dominic asked.

"I hope so. I am going to take him a little way off. Get a fire going while we're gone. A small one, but it's cold and we will need the warmth. And examine yourself for wounds."

Dominic touched his head, where his blond hair was matted with blood, and winced. He nodded, though.

"Just this, and it's from the tree," Dominic said. "No lycanthropy curse. Twice was enough for me. But check yourself, too. The Bitch fucked up your ribs pretty bad."

"I have healed as much of the damage as I can," Jun told him. "But I will need my remaining chi to help Stefano."

"Are you taking him to a ley line?"

Jun shook her head. "The nearest one is hours back the way we came. I don't want to get that separated in case the Bitch returns."

"Where are you going, then?" Dominic asked.

"Just far enough for a little privacy." Jun stood and touched my shoulder. "Stefano, come with me."

Two reflections of the geomancer loomed over me, side by side and shimmering like mirages. I shook my head, trying to clear it, but Jun must have thought I was responding to her.

"I won't hurt you," she promised.

"I know," I said.

I rose unsteadily. Jun took my hand as I reeled, holding me close beside her.

"Please help him," Dominic said.

Jun had to lead me through the forest. I tripped over real roots and bushes that I couldn't see and tried to pull away from imagined shadows. I don't know how long we walked – minutes or days or years. The sun seemed to rise and set, then roll backward across the sky, all without ever banishing the cold black night. I squeezed my eyes shut like a child trying to keep the monster under his bed at bay.

"Stefano? Can you hear me?" Jun asked.

"Yes," I mumbled. "None of it's real. I know that. It's just... just the spell backlash..."

Not that such knowledge would save my sanity now. My grasp on reality was already a tenuous, crumbling thing. But I opened my eyes. Jun had stopped us in a patch of pale moonlight. Gently, she tightened her hand around mine. She seemed to be blushing. Or was that only another hallucination?

"Stefano, I need you to get undressed," Jun told me.

"Uh... what?" I asked. Apparently, I was having auditory hallucinations now.

"I need access to your chakras," Jun said and then offered me a faltering smile. "It's your turn. You had me take off all my clothes when we met, remember?"

I did. At least, I was pretty sure that I remembered Jun standing naked and lovely in front of a fire, her hair wild. If it was just my fraying imagination running away with me, fine. It was better than visions of blood and death.

Jun helped me struggle out of my clothes. The skin tightened across my body and goosebumps prickled my flesh. Jun guided me down into a kneeling position on the forest floor.

"It's cold," I gasped.

The geomancer did something I couldn't see, but the air around me grew a little warmer. Not as warm as sitting beside a fire, but my breath stopped steaming and the goosebumps faded.

Jun sat behind me and I felt her hand against my back. Her fingers traced the blades of my shoulders. I shuddered and gasped again at her touch.

"Still cold?" Jun asked.

"No," I said.

Her hand moved up to the nape of my neck, lingered there for a moment, then trailed slowly down to the base of my spine. My sacrum, if you want to be technical. My ass, if you want to know why I jumped.

"Your meridians are all tangled," Jun said. "Especially the sixth chakra."

"I don't know what that means," I admitted.

"The sixth chakra is the center of insight. The backlash of your spell has cast it into disarray and you can no longer separate truth from delusion."

"I could have told you that."

Jun laughed quietly. She caressed my spine again, her fingers moving slowly along my skin. Despite the warmth she had created, my goosebumps were back.

"I will attempt to cleanse the damage to your sixth chakra," Jun told me. "But I am no master. I could attempt to reroute the power of a ley line through your body, if I could reach one. But that would be like pouring a river through a straw. I could burn out your meridians."

"That sounds bad," I said.

"I have to use my own chi. It is gentler, but I will need to start at the root chakra and work my way up. I'm not skilled enough to jump right to your sixth. And this still might not fix what is wrong with you."

I looked down into my hands. Molten silver was spilling from the pores of my skin and pooling in my palms. We didn't have time to wait for this to pass, if it did at all. Once my illusion of Baba Yaga ran its course, the Bitch would either circle back to take out my team or press on through the mountains to ravage an entire town. I couldn't let either of those things happen.

"Do what you need to do," I said.

Jun grabbed my ass and I jumped. She leaned against my back and I felt her breath warm on the side of my neck.

"Relax," she told me. "This is the first chakra, the root. I have to begin here."

I nodded and exhaled. "How bad is the damage to the rest of my chakras?"

"You don't know?" Jun asked. "Has this never happened to you before?"

Gods, her lips were so close to my ear. I felt them brush against my skin with every word and it was hard to breathe.

"Not to this extent," I said. "Sylvia was a better teacher than that. She would skin me if she saw how sloppy that illusion was."

The trees reached for me with long-clawed hands and my jaw clenched, biting down on the panicked shout that wanted to escape. Jun's strong fingers traced small, intricate patterns at the base of my spine.

The geomancer's touch was so solid, so real. I never realized how good *real* could be. I managed to relax enough to breathe normally again. Well, as normally as I could in the middle of a forest with a beautiful woman grabbing my ass.

"Your first chakra is... ah... very firm," Jun said. "That is the base of the pillar and the seat of strength."

I snorted a short laugh at the sound of that. Jun swatted the back of my head with her free hand.

"This is serious," the geomancer told me, but I heard the smile in her voice. "Concentrate. Your first chakra is strong because you are, Stefano. But you will need that strength to get through the night. Are you ready?"

Ready for what? But before I could ask, Jun pressed the palms of both hands hard against my sacrum. I felt something almost like an electric shock, but it wasn't just a single jolt – it kept burning and didn't fade. There was energy moving through me that was not my own.

"Are you alright?" Jun asked.

"Yes," I gasped. "Keep going."

Her hands moved up along my spine. The hot pressure followed her touch through my body. I gasped again as blood pounded in my ears and rushed between my legs.

"I'm moving to the second chakra," Jun said. "This is the source of pleasure."

Sweat broke out across my face and chest. It rolled down my skin in droplets and left trails of burning sensation in their wake. I groaned and gripped my knees hard enough to bruise them. I was uncontrollably and frighteningly aroused. But so was... someone else? Jun. She said she was using her own chi to repair the damage of my magical backlash. Was that her I felt within me?

"Oh," Jun whispered. Her palms remained pressed against my back. "Stefano?"

"I'm fine," I panted. "Keep going!"

"Nothing wrong with the second chakra. Nothing at all," said the geomancer. "Um... where was I?"

Jun moved another handspan up along my spine and I sensed a fierceness that tasted like her, except that *taste* wasn't the right sense for it. But I felt Jun's hard resolve the same way I knew my own.

"The third chakra is here, in the stomach," she said. "And is elementally associated with fire."

"What's in there?" I asked.

"Willpower. Your drive and your purpose."

And hers. I felt the strength of Jun's spirit, the tenacity that kept her in Les Krovi even after losing everyone and everything else. I remembered her beside the fire again, proud and unflinching under my gaze. I remembered Jun's determination to continue the hunt, with or without my help.

I felt her admiration for my resolve, too, my willingness to endure any danger to take the Bitch and her pack alive. That singular purpose that drove me away from so many people... There was pain in that, but also power.

"The fourth chakra is the source of love," Jun said softly. "And of grief."

Her fingers slid up between my shoulders and I choked on the surge of emotion. I heard my father's scream and the roar of the werewolf that killed him. I saw my mother raging inside her truck, pinned through the chest by the broken steering column. I felt the knife in my hand, the one I used to kill her.

I saw the body of the gray werewolf fall, my bullet in his brain. My hands slipped off my knees and I sagged forward. I barely managed to catch myself with my palms against the earth. Tears burned down my cheeks and caught in my beard.

"I'm sorry, Stefano," Jun said. "I am so sorry you had to kill that man."

"He was a victim." My throat was tight and I struggled to speak at all. "I wanted... I wanted to save him."

"I know."

I felt Jun's head bow until her forehead touched my bare shoulder. Her hair tickled across my skin and her breath was uneven. Jun was crying, too.

"Your heart chakra is damaged," she told me in a faltering voice. "But most of it is old scars."

"Can we skip it, then?"

"No."

I squeezed my eyes shut.

"Then just... just keep going," I said.

Jun's hands shifted, rubbing gently across my shoulders and I felt my mother's arms around me. I smelled my father's aftershave. There was the bright red flash of Lilith in my memories, and the warmth of knowing she would always be there when I called, even if I would never be in her bed again. There was something sharper and harder, something that felt like Sylvia's pride in an accomplished student.

Apparently, my heart wasn't quite as empty as I always thought it was. I curled my fingers into the cold dirt to steady myself. Pain and grief had driven every moment of my life since I was sixteen, but Jun forced me to see more than that.

And I felt her there, too – a kind of magical echo of Jun inside me, maybe left by the chi she poured through my body. After all, Jun couldn't have found a place in my heart so quickly... could she?

The feeling was something like the *Lover's Embrace*, but that spell only connected physical sensation, not emotions. Even when Jun's hands moved up to the back of my neck, though, the warm weight of her in my heart didn't fade.

"The fifth is the chakra of truth," Jun said. Her thumbs massaged up and down the tight muscles in my neck. "It's not quite as battle-scarred as your heart, but there is a lot of healing to be done here, too."

"From the spell?" I asked.

"No, just the same sort of lying to yourself that we all do," Jun said. "Like this shit about needing to work alone."

"I always work alone."

The words were automatic. I had been repeating them endlessly for the last week. But they rang hollow... Lilith had said once that we were a great team. And she was right. I could hunt alone and I was good at it, but I was even better with a team.

Without Jun and Dominic there beside me, I would have died today. The Bitch would have been free to destroy an entire town. We still hadn't stopped her from doing that, but if I had any chance at all of finishing this hunt, both of my partners would be crucial. I couldn't do this without Jun and Dominic.

I cleared my throat.

"Can we... ah... keep going?"

Through our mingled chi, I felt Jun's amusement at my embarrassment. But she slid her fingers up into my hair, cradling the back of my head in gentle hands.

"The sixth chakra," Jun said. "The light chakra. Ah, here is the problem... Tā mā de!"

My head spun and had I been standing, I would have fallen over like a gunshot victim.

I felt sick. Even kneeling on the ground, I fought to remain upright as colors and darkness stormed behind my closed eyelids. Faces rose and fell out of the hurricane, bleeding into one another and then vanishing, only to be replaced by a forest of monstrous bones and spreading branches made of pulsing blood vessels.

I screamed and Jun had to hold me against her. Colorless lights and formless shapes assaulted me, violently nonsensical. This was madness. Bedlam. My illusion spell had folded vision back on itself over and over again. My mind was two broken mirrors facing each other, reflecting a shattered infinity.

Jun cried out. I knew that was my name on her lips – I tasted it like a kiss. But I couldn't hear her. I couldn't see, I couldn't... I felt Jun, though. There was that echo of her heart beating inside me, steady and strong. Horrors surged and swirled, but Jun plucked at one thread and then another until each nightmare unraveled. Her power poured through me, up through my chakras, and pushed the madness away.

I saw the two of us kneeling in the woods, like I floated somehow outside my body. I slumped naked against Jun, utterly helpless in her arms. Moonlight filtered through the trees, dappling our skin in streaks of silver and pewter. Was I still breathing...?

"Stefano," Jun whispered. "Come back."

My vision spun one last time and I fell as if from a great height, back into myself once more.

Slowly, I opened my eyes. Around us, Les Krovi stood motionless and silent in the moonlight. No more phantoms chased each other through my vision. I leaned there bonelessly against Jun and her fingers were still in my hair, stroking gently. She froze when I stirred.

"Sorry," Jun said, starting to back away from me.

"No... wait."

I expected my body to be sore, to protest everything I had just put it through. But I felt... amazing. I turned to Jun and caught her wrist, holding it between us, and ran my thumb across the back of her hand. Her fine bones and soft skin seemed so delicate, but I knew better. I had experienced Jun's strength flowing through me. That was no hallucination and I would never forget it.

Slowly, I raised Jun's hand and kissed her knuckles. They were scuffed and roughened by fighting the Bitch's pack. I kept my eyes closed. I've never been good with women. My obsession, the demands of my trade and my hunt... they have always made it easy to push people away.

I didn't dare watch Jun's face and guess if her smile was mocking or kind, flirtatious or forced. I was afraid to feel her warm and intangible presence inside my heart. I didn't want to think about the fear, that anything I loved could be torn away from me.

Jun held her breath. Her hand trembled in mine, but she didn't pull back.

To hell with it. Fuck fear and fuck caution. For the first time in my life, I wanted something more than I wanted to hunt werewolves. So I tightened my fingers around Jun's slender wrist and pulled her in close. I wrapped my other arm around her waist. The geomancer pressed her body hard against me, turning her face up to mine.

I crushed my lips to hers in a desperate, hungry kiss. Jun wound her arms around me and tangled her fingers into my hair again. Her lips were soft and sweet, her breath hot and coming in swift gasps. Jun's tongue twined with mine, tasting my desire.

"I want you," I panted against her eager mouth. "I need you."

She moaned into the kiss. Jun had explored my very soul and knew what that admission cost me. I had spent every day since I was sixteen trying not to need anyone. But I was so tired of being alone, of keeping my heart in a cage like a dangerous wild animal. It *was* dangerous... I could get hurt and so could Jun. She was tough, though. Tough and brave, intelligent and beautiful.

"I want you, Stefano," Jun whispered into my ear.

I shivered in a way that had nothing to do with the cold Russian night. I wasn't sure what sort of chi manipulation Jun had done to hold the chill at bay, but I doubt that I would have noticed a blizzard right then.

Jun kissed me again, deep and as sweet as honey. Her fingers trailed down over my bare back, nails raking lightly along my skin. There was no healing in her touch now, but there was heat that burned like stars – and fire that rose inside me to answer.

My arms tightened around Jun, trying in vain to pull the geomancer even closer to me. I twisted my fist into the tatters of her shirt and yanked. The cloth tore with a soft sound and I flung it off into the darkness. Jun's nipples were hard points against my chest. They felt so good, but I needed more.

I grabbed Jun's shoulders and drew her back. She whimpered and resisted for a moment, going as immovable as a mountain in my grip. But then her beautiful dark eyes opened and Jun let me hold her just a few inches away, arching her spine so I could drink in the sight of her.

Moonlight glowed silver over the lines of tattoos along the geomancer's arms. Her chest was flushed by desire, small breasts rising and falling in time with her panting breath. I slid a finger across her taut stomach, traced a slow circle around the shallow dip of her navel, then up over her chest. Jun moaned.

I cradled the swell of one breast in my hand and she moaned louder. When I ran my thumb across the perfect peak of her nipple, Jun cried out.

She writhed urgently in my arms, fumbling at the front of her pants. I pulled Jun back against me, grabbed her waistband and yanked them down. The geomancer gasped and bit the side of my neck, just below my ear. Somehow, we managed to kick her pants and shoes away without letting go of each other.

I kissed Jun's throat, feeling her swift pulse flutter against my lips, and then worked my way down to her delicate collarbone. My mouth followed the blush spreading across her chest, over the soft curves of her breasts and finally kissed one dark, hard nipple. Jun squeaked again and grabbed a fistful of my hair, holding me to her.

I devoured the geomancer with a hunger I had never felt before. I bit gently at her silky flesh and then sucked Jun's nipple into my mouth. My beard was rough against her skin, but I flicked my tongue across her sensitive nub in swift, light strokes. Jun shivered and gasped.

"I... I want you to taste me..." she breathed.

"Yes," I said. "Gods, yes."

Jun pulled us both to the ground in a slick, sweaty knot of limbs, maneuvering herself on top of me so gracefully and easily that I half wondered if her chi still connected us. Jun slid along my body and I kissed every inch offered as she moved: the arch of her ribs, her smooth stomach, the crest of her narrow hips. When Jun had finished repositioning herself on top of and opposite me, she parted trembling thighs over my face, opening herself to my ravenous gaze.

I ran my fingers up along Jun's legs, tracing the shining columns of ink on either side of my head, and grabbed her supple ass in both hands. She was facing away, bent over me, but I didn't need to see her expression to know how much Jun wanted this. I could feel it inside me like I felt hunger, and we were both starving.

For a moment, I simply drank in the sight of Jun, her pussy slick and dripping with desire. I curled my fingers around her hips and pulled her down against my waiting lips. I kissed her desperately, along the soft length of her slit and then the wet heat inside.

I didn't know much about the geomancers' magic and nothing about what they might use in bed, but Sylvia had spent years instructing me on how to please a woman. So I applied every lesson she taught me with determination. I wanted to make Jun cum like I had never wanted anything in my life.

Jun straddled my face with her hands braced against my stomach. She threw her head back – I caught a brief glimpse of her long black braid whipping through the starlit night – and moaned something in Mandarin that made me suddenly eager to better learn her language.

And then I was the one gasping as Jun grabbed my cock. Fuck, I hadn't been this hard in a long time... Her fingers were too small to encircle the entire shaft, but I didn't care one bit. Jun's touch made my blood burn and my dick ache for release.

"I want to taste you, too," she said.

My mouth was full of soft flesh and wet juices, so I slid a hand up Jun's tattooed back and seized her braid. Wordlessly, I pushed her head down and lifted my hips, hoping she understood my need.

She did. Jun moaned and her warm lips closed around my cock. I groaned against her pussy and Jun swallowed me deeper. Her tongue worked over me, tracing hot lines of pleasure along my length. I held her braid loosely as we devoured each other, showing Jun how badly I wanted her mouth on my dick, but letting her set the pace and depth. It was intensely erotic, holding Jun's hair and feeling her head bob up and down on me.

I nuzzled my face between her legs, exploring Jun with my tongue and lips to find the places that made her moan the loudest. She struggled to swallow my cock deeper in response, stifling her cries on my hardness. I released Jun's braid to grab her ass in both hands and run the flat of my tongue over her swollen little clitoris. Jun's voice rose to a ringing cry.

I moved my hands along the smooth curve of her ass and down her thighs. The muscles were tight and skin slicked by dripping wetness. Jun's mouth popped off my cock with a sharp smack and she gasped for air.

"Yes!" she cried. "More... more, Stefano... Don't stop!"

I had no intention of stopping. Nothing else in the worlds mattered but Jun's pleasure. I circled her clit with my tongue, licking hard back and forth. Jun trembled on top of me and grabbed the base of my cock in one hand. I thought she was only seizing a handhold, but the young geomancer would not be so easily outdone.

Jun stuffed my dick between her lips, gagging herself on my length just as she started to scream. I felt the sound of it against my skin, playing over my every nerve like a bow across violin strings. It felt... perfect. Jun's tongue lashed frantically along my cock, devouring me with an urgency that made my heart pound. That made my blood boil and my balls churn.

I groaned, wanting to warn Jun. But I couldn't do it with words – that would require removing my lips from her soft, sweet skin. Her pussy tightened as my hips jerked helplessly. Jun knew what was coming and swallowed me deep to take the first great spume of my load.

I grabbed her ass hard and held on as thick, hot ecstasy coursed through my entire body and poured into Jun's mouth. Her tongue never stopped moving and the geomancer writhed against me.

Gods, it was glorious. I kissed and licked Jun's streaming pussy, tasting her pleasure as I gushed my own down her throat in a perfect cycle – her into me, me into her.

Only after I had pumped what felt like a gallon of cum into Jun's mouth did I finally release her. She sat up slowly, sucking down every last drop of semen as she pulled her lips off of my cock with a wet noise. Her pussy dripped when she drew away and the taste of her was sweet on my tongue.

Jun swung her leg up and off, giving me room to sit. Her chest was heaving and glistened with sweat. A slick line of white ran from one corner of her mouth, pale in the moonlight. Jun wiped it off on the back of her hand, then licked my cum from her skin and swallowed with a soft sound of satisfaction.

Jun opened her eyes and saw me staring. I hooked one arm around her waist, pulling her close again. She grabbed my shoulders and crushed her lips to mine in a long, deep kiss that tasted of our mingled pleasure.

"That was..." Jun couldn't seem to find the words.

"Yes," I agreed breathlessly.

"I want... I need more."

"Good," I growled. "So do I."

"There are things I can do," Jun said. "Magic that affects the second chakra, if you want..."

I traced the sharp angle of her jaw and then touched my thumb against her lips, silencing Jun. I had my own magic, too, passion charms in my wallet that would keep me rock-hard all night.

But I didn't want her magic or mine right now. I just wanted Jun. Just her beauty and strength, her intelligence and her fierce determination.

I pulled Jun tight against me, eliciting a soft moan from the geomancer, and lowered her slowly down into the moss and leaves. She spread her slender legs before me and twined them about my waist in a trembling embrace. Jun reached one slim hand between our bodies, curling her fingers around my cock. I was still gloriously, painfully hard and groaned at her touch.

Jun guided me and I sank my dick slowly, inch by inch, into the yielding heat of her. Gods, she was wet. Dripping. Jun was so much smaller than I was, but I slid easily into her and we both gasped at the sweet sensation.

"Oh," Jun whimpered. "Stefano, yes...!"

Her eyes were wide and fever-bright. I held Jun tight to me as she writhed against my body and pressed her heels to the small of my back. I drew my hips away and then pushed forward again into Jun. Her spine arched as I filled her again.

Jun wound her arms around me and then the soft touch of her nimble fingers moved down my back, feeling out each muscle flexing as I worked in and out of her.

I didn't dare close my eyes. I couldn't bear to miss a moment of this. There were leaves in Jun's hair and stony earth under my knees, but I didn't care. We didn't need a bed to make it perfect.

We started slow, but neither of us could hold ourselves back. Even pinned beneath me, Jun raised her hips to meet my thrusts, pushing herself against the ground to work herself desperately up and down my dick. She was tight and wet and silky soft inside... I pounded myself into Jun so hard that I was driving us back across the moonlit clearing. If we had been in a bed, I would have fucked her right through the headboard by now.

Jun gasped and moaned in swift Mandarin. I didn't need to understand the words – I understood how her body tightened against mine, how her pussy squeezed around my cock. She was cumming. Wetness streamed along my dick and spattered the forest floor beneath us in glittering drops.

My heart pounded a swift tempo through me that demanded more. *Faster, deeper, harder...!* I held Jun against my chest and surged up to my knees on the leaf-strewn ground. Her legs tightened instinctively around my waist as I lifted her up. But I cradled Jun in my arms, suspending her on the steely length of my dick.

"Stefano!" she gasped.

I held Jun there and drove my cock up into her slender body. She threw back her head, haloed in wild black hair, and clung to me as I fucked her hard. Her breasts bounced with every thrust and Jun's voice broke, becoming a silent scream of pleasure.

I never wanted it to end. I just wanted to stay there forever, sunk to the hilt inside the beautiful geomancer, tangled together in the moonlight. My world was madness all over again – a horizon of smooth skin and tattooed quicksilver stars, a sea of perfect soft wetness gripping me and a supernova sun of searing ecstasy.

Jun twined her fingers through my hair and pulled me into a soul-deep kiss. I bore her to the ground again and drowned in the taste of her. I drove myself into Jun once and then twice more. She was trembling, biting my lower lip as she came on the end of my cock. Her pussy milked me frantically and her heart hammered fast against mine where our bodies pressed together into one.

Jun swallowed a hasty breath and finally found her voice. "I... I want your cum."

The whole world spun. With an effort that made me growl like a werewolf, I yanked my cock out of Jun. Kedra had wanted a child, but even through the storm of pleasure consuming me, I didn't want to risk fucking up Jun's life.

My dick shone wetly in the cold moonlight, as shiny and silver as the geomancer's tattoos. Drops splashed against her thighs and I reached for the slick shaft, but Jun was faster. Her hand shot out like a lightning strike and grabbed my cock in strong fingers.

She stroked me just once, from root to tip. That was all it took. The pleasure of Jun's touch was electric and my cum flew out in a shockingly pale streak all the way to her breastbone. Jun jerked me and more pearls of white beaded her heaving chest. Another liquid line sprayed across her stomach and pooled like cream in her navel. Jun's expression was one of fierce concentration as she coaxed every last drop from me.

Jun released my cock and stared down in wonderment at the mess I had made. She ran her fingers through the thick puddle, tracing out lines and symbols that meant nothing... but were still magical right at that moment. I sat up straight and drew a deep breath that tasted and smelled like sex. Like us.

"We need to get back to Dominic," I said.

"Yes," Jun agreed with a small sigh. "Probably."

I stood and found our clothes. Jun's shirt was torn far beyond repair, but I held it out and she used the rags to scrub my sticky mess from her skin. When Jun was done, I offered her my hand.

"I would like to try out your magic," I said. "And maybe show you some of mine next time."

Jun's eyes widened. "Next time?"

"If you want there to be a next time."

I craved more. Not only more sex – though I was already eager for another taste of Jun's pussy – but more of *her*. Jun smiled up at me, then twined her fingers into mine.

"It's a date," she said.

I helped Jun up to her feet and she stood up on her toes to kiss me. The kiss threatened to go on too long and send us right down to the ground in a sweaty knot again. But I managed to stop, panting, and offer my shirt to Jun.

"Since I ruined yours," I said.

Jun pulled my shirt on over her head and grinned at me. "You know, I stopped you from fucking Kedra's ass. I feel like I owe you."

My brows shot up and I nearly dropped my pants. Jun laughed brightly.

"Next time," she said.

Chapter
FIFTEEN

Dominic was already on his feet when we returned to our little camp. He gripped his shotgun in white-knuckled fists, but dropped the muzzle toward the ground and replaced the safety.

"Leaves in your hair, dirt on your clothes, shit-eating grins..." Dominic noted. "Not to mention those sounds I heard. I'm guessing Stefano is feeling a lot better."

Jun blushed and I knew that I was turning red too, but I nodded. Dominic had washed the blood from his scalp and now his wet blond hair stuck to the side of his face.

"Yes," I answered. "Jun used her chi to repair the damage to my mind."

I went to my pack and took out a fresh shirt, dressed again, then pulled my coat back on. Without Jun warming the air, Les Krovi was bitterly cold once more. I sat down next to a small alcohol gel burner that Dominic had set up. A bowl of soup simmered over the blue flame.

Jun sat beside me. After all of the chi she had expended fighting the werewolves, healing herself and then me, the geomancer was probably running pretty damn low. My shirt was warmer than the rags Jun had been wearing, but I put an arm around her and the gesture didn't go unnoticed.

"So is it safe to assume that you've checked each other over for werewolf injuries?" Dominic asked with a grin.

To my mixed horror and pleasure, Jun smirked right back.

"Every inch," she answered. "Several wounds, but none left by tooth or claw."

"Well, unless you have a sister to take a look at me, I had to check myself," said Dominic. "I'm all clear, too."

"I have three sisters, actually," Jun told him.

"How's your hand?" I asked.

Dominic wrenched his wide green eyes off Jun and turned to me. He held up his left hand. The skin there was angry and red with chemical burns.

"I was sweating," Dominic said. "Sorry, Stefano."

Lye was solid, a plain white powder. On dry skin, it could be easily cleaned away. But lye reacted violently with water, including sweat. And Dominic had just been running away from a pack of werewolves.

I took Dominic's hand carefully and inspected the damage. The burns were small, but they were bad. It didn't look like he had tried to quell the chemical reaction with vinegar. Yes, I've seen movies and yes, I was worried that Dominic had hurt himself worse by following cinematic advice. Vinegar *did* neutralize lye, but the reaction was fiercely exothermic. Which meant that it only made the burn worse.

"Can you move your fingers?" I asked.

Dominic clenched his left hand into a fist, but he hissed in pain. Jun looked over my shoulder, worry on her face.

"How bad is it?" Dominic asked.

"Nothing every wizard hasn't done a dozen times," I said.

I released Dominic's hand and pulled my backpack open. I found the sealed plastic bag of willow bark and took out two strips, then drew the activating runes on each piece in burdock charcoal. After I had passed my hand over them, speaking the short incantation, I held the bark out to Dominic.

"Take one now," I instructed. "And then the second in about an hour."

Dominic put a bark strip in his mouth and began chewing. I knew from a lot of experience that the healing spell tasted like shit, but his burns would be gone by morning. Dominic swallowed without complaint and flexed the fingers of his left hand.

"It already hurts less," he said. "Thanks, boss."

I prepared another strip of willow bark while Jun checked on the soup and poured it into three cups. She passed them out to each of us and I gave her the other healing spell. She hadn't protested at all when we were fucking in the moonlight – quite the opposite, in fact – but Jun had healed me and I wanted to return the favor.

She took the piece of inscribed willow bark and sat next to me again while we drank our soup. I recognized the bowl that had been used to heat dinner, though. Dominic had lined it in a double layer of aluminum foil, but that was one of the bowls I used for mixing up dry spell components.

Dominic caught my look, then sighed and combed his uninjured hand through tangled blond hair.

"Sorry," he said. "I had to make do. We lost half our shit when we ran."

I glanced around the tiny makeshift camp. My backpack was the only one. Dominic had removed his while making the Janus mixture for my illusion spell and had no time to collect it again before we escaped. Unless we went back for them, half of our supplies were simply gone.

"I... I'm really sorry, Stefano," Dominic told me. He held his soup mug tightly, not drinking. "About... everything. I fucked it all up. Bad."

"It's okay," I said. "You did well. Both of you."

Dominic looked like I had just dropped a bomb on him, but a grin spread slowly across his face. Jun smiled, too, and put her hand on my thigh.

"We failed tonight," she said. "But our hunt is not over."

"What's next?" Dominic asked.

They both looked at me. I set my soup down on my knee and scratched my beard, thinking. An icy wind whipped through the pine trees, making wood creak and groan. I listened for howls, but didn't hear anything unnatural.

"Luring one werewolf away at a time won't work again," I said. "The Bitch is too smart to let us pull the same trick twice. She set a trap for us and understood our magic well enough to spring it in an area with no ley lines."

Dominic nodded. "She spoke, too. I'm not confirming anything, but I might have peed a little."

"It's not simply that the Bitch spoke. It's what she said. That was grief. Grief for the werewolf that... that I killed."

I had to pause and swallow a painful lump in my throat. Jun put her arm around me. Dominic's expression fell and he opened his mouth to apologize again.

"Stop," I told him. "It's *not* your fault."

"It's not yours, either," Dominic said. He held my gaze until I finally nodded.

"Where is the Bitch now?" Jun asked. "She's not close enough for me to sense."

I found the box of grave dirt in my backpack and unfurled the bronze pendulum from inside. Thankfully, all of the components for the dowsing had been stored in my pack, already pre-measured and ready for mixing. Dominic offered to take care of the blood rune, but I shook my head.

"You've lost enough blood for one day," I told him.

I ran my knife through the flame of the alcohol burner to sterilize the blade, then nicked the back of my hand. With a couple beads of blood, I painted the dagaz rune on two faces of the crystal. When it was dry, Dominic held out the pendulum, already filled with ash and zaffre. I sealed it, completed the incantation, and then flicked the pendulum carefully into motion. It swung out to the northeast.

"The Bitch is heading for the town again," Jun said. "She is done wasting time with us."

Or maybe the Bitch's need was that much more urgent now. But her need for what, exactly? To wipe out some Russian village? That didn't make any sense.

"Werewolves have a soul-deep hatred for all Merlinic magic," I said. "Ever since Merlin used that magic to seal the demons away in the Nether."

"That's why they always come after you, right?" Dominic asked.

I nodded. "Until now. But what could possibly be more important to the Bitch than killing us?"

"Especially when you have already stolen away two members of her pack," Jun said.

"Why a pack of five?" I asked, only half to myself. "Sylvia said that the Bitch always brings her pack to five. She had a family, before her change. A husband and three children."

"A family of five," Jun said. "You think that the Bitch has recreated her family? The one she lost?"

"Werewolves are driven by their passions. Anger and hunger. Perhaps love and loss, too."

"Love?" Dominic asked. "Dude, she was beating the shit out of those other werewolves!"

"She's cursed," I reminded him. "That curse is demonic and demons corrupt a lot more than the body. You know that better than most. They can twist the soul, too. But the Bitch still remembers her family."

"Do you think she is trying to replace the ones we took?" Jun asked. "To restore her pack to five?"

I shook my head. "We only started reducing her numbers yesterday. The Bitch has been on this path ever since we arrived in Les Krovi. I think that town was always her destination."

"Why?" Jun asked. "Just to kill more humans?"

"I'm... not sure," I admitted. "Werewolves are wild and destructive. But they're almost impossible to control, even for demons. They're not particular about what they kill – deer are just as good as humans, as long as they bleed. Why travel so far only to attack a town? There are thousands of acres of taiga in every direction."

"Uh," said Dominic. "Stop me if this sounds stupid... but I was a werewolf. Twice. I don't remember much, but I remember the rage. Everything was just this red haze. I wanted to kill... everyone. And I tried to do it. I really did."

Dominic stared into his rapidly cooling soup. He still hadn't touched it. The boy knew he wasn't at fault for what he had done while he was a werewolf. He didn't even remember it. But that didn't stop it from hurting, I supposed. Dominic told me that he was out here to help, and I believed him. But maybe he was trying to atone for the lives he had taken, too.

Jun and I sat quietly, waiting for Dominic to go on.

"But the rage never stopped," he said eventually. "There's never enough of anything for a werewolf. Not enough blood or pain or destruction. The Bitch has always had a pack, right?"

I nodded.

"So what if it's not enough for her anymore?" Dominic asked. "I mean, the other werewolves are all gone. They've all been hunted down and cured. It's just the Bitch and her pack now."

Shit. Dominic was right – the Bitch needed a larger pack. A bigger family.

"How many people did you say are in that town?" I asked Jun.

"About a thousand."

One in twenty werewolf victims survived to be changed by the curse. In a town of a thousand, that was fifty new lycanthropes.

But Sylvia said that the Bitch's unprecedented self-control extended to wounding instead of killing, drastically increasing her victim's odds of survival and transformation. A conservative estimate of the Bitch's restraint – and how well she was able to control the rest of her pack – would quadruple the conversion rate.

A thousand people was a small town, a remote and rural one. There was no way they could fight off the Bitch. Eight hundred people would die. Two hundred more would become werewolves. I came to Russia to end lycanthropy and found myself facing an epidemic. No magical force on Earth could stop an army of two hundred werewolves. They would rage across the world, killing and converting millions.

I wasn't going to let that happen.

I found the map in one of my pockets and unfolded it across my knee. It was a little more rumpled than before, but still legible. The alcohol gel was burning low, so Dominic grabbed a flashlight from my backpack and held it out over the map.

"So what are we going to do?" Dominic asked. "Can we get the Castle to evacuate the town or something?"

"Maybe," I answered. "But action on that scale will get Baba Yaga's attention. The Castle *might* be able to negotiate with her, but that will take time that we don't have. We've got one shot to teleport the remaining pack."

"You mean all of them at once?" Dominic asked.

"We need to trap all three in one teleportation circle," I said.

Dominic almost dropped the flashlight. "But I... I thought we weren't going to try that. I mean, you have to be in that circle too, don't you?"

I nodded.

"Jun, just how big are Stefano's balls?" Dominic asked.

The geomancer made a show of not answering the question, but she was completely failing to conceal a smirk. I coughed and moved hastily on.

"The Bitch likes to keep her pack close," I said. "Especially now, after we've tried to separate them. But now we might be able to make that work in our favor."

"We know the town's location and the direction the Bitch will approach from," Jun added. "We can lay a trap ahead of them."

Dominic nodded. "Before they can get in there and start their rampage. Okay, sounds good. But how are we going to do that? The Bitch moves a hell of a lot faster than we do."

"I might be able to run fast enough," Jun said. "If I can find a strong ley line to follow. There are several near the town. But I can't carry both of you."

"Dominic?" I asked.

"Yeah?"

"Can I teleport us close to the town? Do we have the reagents?"

"Uh... My phone is dead and I lost the solar charger back there," Dominic said, pointing back in the general direction of the logging road. He glanced at my pack and I could see him running through the math in his head. "But I kept the teleportation shit divided between us, since you carry so much of it. With two extra spell targets, you have reagents left for... three castings."

"Enough to get us there, to teleport the pack, and then get back to the Castle," I said.

"I can measure it all out," Dominic offered. "I'll uh... need to use your tools, though. All of mine are gone."

"Sure," I said with a nod. "Get started. And check the case at the bottom of my backpack. There should be a spare gun in there, too. I... left mine on the road."

Jun had taken the map from my hand at some point, so deftly that I failed to notice until she held it out toward me. She tapped her finger on the western edge of the village sketched there.

"The forest has been cleared away for nearly a mile around the town. The people there will see what we are doing," Jun said. "And they will see the werewolves."

"But we can wipe their memories later, right?" Dominic asked.

"Even if we have enough belladonna for that, we don't want a bunch of untrained civilians blundering into the middle of a hunt," I said. "They don't know what they're doing. We do."

Dominic blinked. "We?"

"Yes," I said. "Now, there's a sort of ward I can cast that will keep anyone from noticing what's going on beyond it. The Bitch could bring a marching band and no one would even look twice."

"Uh, *Evaine's Glass*?" Dominic asked. "But the willow rods are gone. They were all in my backpack."

I rubbed my jaw. Jun seemed to find the process intensely fascinating and I flushed. I needed to trim my beard again...

"Arctic willow," I said. "We should be far enough north now for it. But the willow here is a shrub, not a tree."

Dominic was shaking his head. "Stefano, you've already had one spell backfire because we weren't properly prepared. Do you think we can really just... make new reagents?"

"There are a thousand lives at stake. We have to *make* it work. The rods need to be charged with six hours of moonlight. So we better get them now or else we're waiting until tomorrow night."

"I don't think the town has that long," Jun said.

We collected another flashlight and headed out into the dark forest. The moon was still high in the sky, but clouds drifted in as we searched, forcing us to rely on the narrow beams of artificial radiance. I was just about to conjure up a more powerful magical spark when Dominic's flashlight passed over a large, pale shrub.

"That's it," I said.

I crouched and cleared away a few wispy ferns. The bush rose about waist-high in a half-dozen slender branches. I inspected the arctic willow and looked up at Dominic and Jun.

"*Evaine's Glass* spell requires five willow rods," I told them. "But only three of these branches are thick enough. Find me another just like it."

Dominic nodded. He and Jun moved slowly in opposite directions, searching for more arctic willows.

I used my knife to cut off the three thickest branches, making myself a trio of four-inch wooden rods. By the time I stripped away the bark, Dominic had located another arctic willow and removed two more branches. He held the flashlight as I trimmed them all down to size, but watched the sky with a frown.

"Those clouds will clear up, won't they?" Dominic asked. "We need that moonlight for your spell."

I finished peeling the bark off the last rod. Jun handed me the other four and I looked up through the trees. The stars and moon had all vanished behind a blanket of gray.

"Not with enough time left to charge the rods," I growled. "We'll need some wind."

"That's serious magic," Dominic said.

"And I'm not very good at weather spells." I pocketed the willow rods and began hiking back in the direction of our camp. "At this altitude, it's going to be hard to move enough air to disperse those clouds... But at least I'm not taking off my clothes this time."

"I didn't ask, dude," said Dominic.

"Aw," Jun muttered.

"I'm not sure we have enough of... anything for weather magic," Dominic said.

Jun fell into step beside me. The short geomancer was smirking. "Well, since the spell does not require you to be naked, why bother with it at all?"

"What have you got in mind?" I asked.

"Moonlight is energy," Jun said. "A form of chi. Merlinic wizards are not the only ones who gather and harness its power. The light is diffuse now, but I can control and focus it into the willow wood."

"You can?" Dominic asked.

"I will take excellent care of Stefano's rod," Jun promised with a perfectly straight face.

Dominic laughed and my face went hot. I spotted the log that was the backdrop of our campsite and headed that direction.

"Thanks, Jun," I said in a slightly strangled voice. "They need exactly six hours of full moonlight to be effective. Can you do that?"

"Easily," Jun answered. The geomancer slowed to a stop a hundred yards outside camp. "I can do it here, where I will not have to filter out any firelight."

Jun took my hand and dragged me to a stop, then stretched up onto her toes to kiss me. I was very conscious of Dominic watching us, but some things are more important than being a stoic badass. I pulled Jun close and returned her kiss. Finally, we had to come up for breath and Jun slipped out of my arms.

"We won't be far away," I told her. "We've got some calculations to do for enlarging the teleportation circles. Dominic, I could use your help."

"You got it, boss."

We continued back toward camp, but I looked over my shoulder to see Jun folding her legs into a lotus position. The rods of arctic willow lay in a row on the ground in front of her like offerings. She pushed up the long sleeves of her shirt – of my shirt – to bare her tattooed arms. The lines of silver ink shone far more brightly than they should have under the dark, clouded sky. Dominic glanced at Jun, too, and held out his fist for a bump.

"You're a lucky man," he whispered.

"I will be if this plan works," I said.

I ignored Dominic's fist-bump and hurried back to camp.

According to a fading hand-painted sign beside the road, the town on the other side of the mountains was named *Belosnezhka*. Small, sturdy houses and shops clustered around a Soviet-era lumber mill that had been converted long ago into some sort of warehouse. A white blanket of fresh snow lay over the town, thin and fragile and already melting as the sun rose to push back the shadow of the mountains. Dawn came early here, but Belosnezhka was awake and bustling. People gathered all along the main road, unloading crates from their trucks and setting up folding tables for what looked like a weekend market.

Dominic shouted and waved his arms back and forth over his head. An old man looked up from a crate of bottled milk, squinted in the wrong direction, and then went back to his business.

"Looks like that's working," said Dominic.

I inspected the golden thread I had knotted around the final willow rod. The wood had been difficult to drive into the frozen ground, but the arctic willow was tough and hardy, and now the rods were all planted in a row like the pickets of a tiny fence.

"*Evaine's Glass* deflects interest," I said. "No one in Belosnezhka should notice what we're up to out here."

"There are only like three roads that leave town. What if some-one needs to use this one?" Dominic asked.

I glanced back along the road. The surface was rough and cratered in deep potholes, with just a few patchy sections of intact asphalt beneath the frost. It was the relic of the logging industry decades gone, but we had been able to travel the road easily enough and I supposed that it probably still saw occasional use. It certainly would today.

"The spell should hold," I said. "Anyone trying to come this way will decide to take their trip tomorrow, or find a reason to leave by another route. Short of a nuclear blast, nothing should turn their attention this way. At least, for a population center of this size."

"So what happens if a bunch of people come from out of town to hit the market?" Dominic asked.

"The strain on the spell is proportional to the number of people it affects," I answered. "The population of Moscow would shatter this ward in seconds. Jun, do you think anyone else is coming?"

The geomancer touched her fingers to the cold, empty air and closed her eyes. "I sense just a few other people outside the town. Farmers, I believe, but I count only twenty of them. Will they affect your spell?"

"Not significantly," I said. "The rest must already be in Belos-nezhka for market day."

"So we're good?" Dominic asked.

I nodded and took the dowsing pendulum from my pocket. It was running low on demonic energy, but it swung out in a short, agitated arc in the direction of the mountains.

"The Bitch is on her way," I said. "Jun, can you sense her?"

She shook her head. "No, not yet. But I should prepare the way before she gets that close. How much room do you need for your teleportation circle?"

"Make it at least twenty-seven feet wide," I answered. "Eight and a half meters."

She nodded and I gestured to Dominic. We moved away. Jun turned her back to the town and raised her arms up overhead. She held that pose for a long moment, perfectly still, and then pushed her hands slowly down toward the ground. The road shuddered beneath my feet.

Jun pivoted up on the ball of one foot and stretched out with arms and legs in the direction of the network of ley lines that ran through the heart of Belosnezhka. The geomancer closed her fingers into fists, grabbing that magical flow, and then pulled. She spun in a graceful circle and lifted both hands. The earth all along the road grumbled, roared and then heaved itself thirty feet into the air. Another swift spin, a low sweep of Jun's leg, and the other side of the road suddenly rose up into a steep three-story embankment.

The citizens of Belosnezhka glanced around at the earthquake with mild puzzlement. But as soon as the ground stilled once more, they lost interest and went back to setting up their market stalls. Fascinating... Either the arctic willow wasn't working quite as well as the *salix exigua* I usually stocked, or else Jun's direct manipulation of the ley lines was partially circumventing my spell. I wished that I had time to study the effect, but we had a more important job to do.

Jun had turned the road into a narrow, high-walled ravine just wide enough for me to cast my teleportation spell. Roots left over from long-felled trees jutted and snaked out from the sides of the impromptu crevasse. Jun made a sharp chopping motion with one hand and the earth closed up around the wood, severing the old gray roots.

"It will never pass for natural," Jun said. "But perhaps the Bitch will not realize quite so quickly that this is a new trap."

She pushed sweaty strands of hair back from her face. Dominic knelt a few feet away, setting out the ingredients for my spell on the largest patch of intact asphalt.

"Sixty-five percent extra cinquefoil and pearlash," Dominic said. "Myrrh, wormwood and blue vitriol – all ready to go."

I triple-checked my pockets to make sure I had enough ebony charcoal. A rough surface like the road would go through it faster, but we were out of the canvas tarps I had laid out in Les Krovi. I chose a stick of inert chalk and glanced up at the sky. The sun was half hidden behind streaks of gray cloud, but the bright glow was still visible enough for me to mark out thirteen and twenty-seven degrees off true north for the extra ehwaz runes.

"And algiz runes for the two additional targets," I muttered to myself, ticking off where they would need to be drawn on the road.

Dominic verified my work with a compass and we made some minor adjustments. We didn't want three werewolves appearing in a single fusion of claws and rage at the Tower. Without the algiz runes, the spell wouldn't be able to differentiate between targets. They would all arrive disastrously in the same space, crushed into a single mass, and we would have saved no one.

"That's all we can do for the moment," I said. "At least until the pack is twelve minutes away."

"So now we wait?" Dominic asked.

I nodded. Dominic paced along the road, checking his shotgun and staring out to the west – the direction that the Bitch and her remaining werewolves would come from. His breath steamed into white plumes in the frigid morning air.

I hunkered down against the edge of the ravine and tried to blow some warmth into my hands. A wizard with numb fingers was a dead one. Jun knelt down next to me and took my hands in hers, squeezing them gently. Heat flowed from her skin and into me.

"Thanks," I said. "Don't waste chi on me, though. You're going to need it."

Jun smiled. "The land here is well-tended and the ley lines are strong. I have more than enough energy. If we had time, I would take you flying."

That sounded like... fun. Informative, too – the geomancers and the Merlinic orders have always had a difficult relationship and we knew only a little about each other's magic. Or even about one another's lives.

Jun's hands were still around mine and she didn't seem in a hurry to remove them. She nodded toward the eastern end of her ravine and the town beyond.

"It is strange to see so many people going about their lives so close," Jun said.

"The ward is working."

"That isn't what I mean," Jun said. She hesitated before going on. "I was the first hostage that Ptah demanded. His first prisoner. I lived inside the walls of his palace for over a year. I spoke to no one that Ptah did not invite there. When he did not require my... attention... I was usually alone."

Jun slipped one of her hands out of mine and ran it up her opposite arm, tracing the line of her tattoos through her sleeve. She shuddered, though I knew for a fact that the geomancer wasn't cold.

"I spent a lot of that lonely time thinking about what I would do when I was free again," Jun said. "When I went back to my life. Ptah did not let me practice my magic, so that was the first thing I did."

She pushed up one sleeve, displaying her quicksilver tattoos this time. Jun must have gotten them only after escaping Ptah. The Egyptian mummy would never have allowed any of his hostages so much power. Asshole.

I glanced at Jun for permission and she dipped her chin once. I ran my fingers over the shining lines of silver. Goosebumps rose along her skin at my touch and Jun bit her lower lip. A bolt of something hot and heavy jolted through my heart and I almost couldn't resist the urge to pull Jun into my arms.

"Now I find myself having lonely thoughts about my future again," Jun said. Her voice was steady, but very quiet. "But what about you, Stefano? What will you do when this is done? When the last werewolf is cured and their curse is gone from our world?"

Jun had seen into my heart when she used her own soul to heal mine. She knew all about my crusade against lycanthropy, what it meant to me. And what it had cost me. The end of the hunt was drawing near – in defeat or victory, I wasn't sure.

What would be left of my life when it was over?

"I... don't know," I admitted. I looked back in the direction of Belosnezhka. "I haven't lived a normal life in a long time. I don't think I would even know how."

"A life does not need to be ordinary to be happy," Jun said. "And maybe it does not have to be lonely."

My throat went tight and my heart raced. Was she...? But Jun jumped to her feet, dark eyes narrowed.

"She is coming," the geomancer hissed. "The Bitch has reached the edge of the forest."

"How many are there?" I asked.

"Three. She has not yet been able to expand her pack."

I pushed myself upright and Dominic ran to my side. I pointed to the two walls of the gorge above.

"Twelve minutes," I told them. "Get the pack coming toward me. Jun, close the exit behind them. Dominic, keep them moving and keep them down in the ravine. Do you have enough silver?"

Dominic patted the bulging pockets of his pants. "Yeah, boss. Twenty shells of extra-shiny buckshot."

"Are you ready?" Jun asked him.

Dominic nodded and stepped back against the sheer wall of the ravine. Jun gathered herself, then lifted one arm in a swift arc. A pillar of earth twisted itself free beneath Dominic and rose from the ground, carrying him up like an elevator.

When he reached the top of the crevasse, Dominic jumped off and flashed me a thumbs-up. Then he dashed west, shotgun held at the ready. With his phone dead, Dominic would have to count out the time while running and gunning against three werewolves.

Jun pressed her lips to mine in a short, desperate kiss. But before I could say a word, the geomancer leapt into the air, her tattoos flashing. Jun flew skyward like a leaf caught in the wind, bounded once off of the ravine wall and then vanished up over the edge.

It was hard to watch them go. But I wasn't alone – one thousand people of Belosnezhka stood at my back and it was time to give them everything I had. So I grabbed salt in my left hand, charcoal in my right, and went to work.

I drew out circles and runes swiftly on the road. Jun's warmth stayed with me and my hands remained steady despite the icy cold. But that didn't stop me from shivering when I heard the Bitch's first savage howl. The sound echoed down the ravine, joined in wild chorus by two more growling and barking voices. Dominic's shotgun cracked and the ground rumbled. That was Jun closing the mouth of the gorge and trapping the pack down here with me... I hoped.

There was no time to worry about the rest of my team. I had to trust Jun and Dominic to do their jobs, like they trusted me. I finished the interlocking runic circles and broke the seal on the pearlash and blue vitriol. The mixture smoked and I burned my final teleportation runes into the broken asphalt.

The sounds of gunshots, howls and the grinding roar of moving earth were getting closer. I stepped into the circle of salt and began my invocation.

"Incoming!" Dominic shouted from above.

I saw the other werewolves first, the white-furred female and the lanky auburn male. Then came the Bitch, her body huge and black and silver and rippling with hundreds of pounds of muscle. The demon wolves charged down the road, eating up the distance between us in great loping strides. Behind them, the ravine pulled shut like a zipper and Jun bounded in aerial leaps across the top, herding the pack in toward my spell.

Dominic ran along the wall on my right, dangerously close to a thirty-foot fall. The white werewolf dropped to all fours and began scrambling up the side of the miniature canyon. It sank hooked claws deep into the earth and climbed. Dominic aimed over the edge and fired, blowing fur and blood from the beast's paw. The pale wolf tumbled back down into the road with a howl.

The Bitch saw me. She felt my spell and her golden eyes blazed with fury. That demonic yellow gaze went to the circle at my feet and there was recognition in her savage expression. The Bitch didn't just sense my magic – she *knew* the spell. Did she remember Sylvia casting it years ago? Her muzzle peeled back from fangs the length of my fingers and the Bitch growled out a deep warning.

"Stop!" she snarled.

The other two werewolves were still chasing Dominic down the ravine, wild with bloodlust. The Bitch lunged forward, catching the white one by the scruff of its neck and flung it back the way they had come. The smaller wolf hit the ground and thrashed upright, growling and snapping.

"Stop!" the Bitch roared again. "Get out!"

The werewolf queen hurled herself forward and closed a huge paw around the cinnamon-colored male's throat. She flung him back away from me, smashing him against the ravine wall with force enough to snap bones. When he tried to rush at me again, the Bitch nipped his flank... a "nip" that tore a raw red chunk of flesh the size of my hand from the other lycanthrope's side.

With howls and savage blows, the Bitch turned her pack around and chased them back toward Jun. Dominic fired a spreading shot of silver down into her massive black-furred back and the Bitch gave a bone-rattling growl. She laid her long ears flat against her skull, but she ignored Dominic and drove the other werewolves ahead of her – away from me and my spell.

Jun jerked to a halt at the suddenly truncated end of the miniature canyon and the ground went still beneath her. She whirled in a tight circle and the slope of earth sealing the ravine slicked itself up into a sheer, flat face. But that would only halt the Bitch's retreat for a minute or two at best – there wasn't much in this world that werewolves couldn't climb.

I didn't dare stop the incantation. The backlash of an illusion spell might drive the caster mad, but butchering a teleportation could tear a hole into the Earth. And I don't mean the ground – failed teleportation magic would leave a bleeding gash in our very plane of existence.

I shot an urgent look up at Dominic. He nodded and scrambled over the edge of Jun's ravine, half skidding and half tumbling down the steep slope toward me. The young man slewed to a stop in a shower of earth and rocks in front of my spell circle and spat out a mouthful of dirt.

"Hey!" Dominic shouted. "Hey, you big bitch! Where the hell do you think you're going?"

He had dropped his gun in the fall and now pulled a folding knife from his pocket. I had no idea if the blade was silvered. But even if it were – and even if it had been a sword instead of a pocket knife – Dominic would have to be insane to think he could go toe-to-toe with a pack of werewolves.

But he didn't try to fight them. Instead, Dominic closed his fingers around the blade, thought better of it, and then slashed the knife across the back of his hand. He clenched his bloody fist and raised it up into the air. Just like me in Louisiana.

"Dinner time!" Dominic announced in a loud voice. "Come and get it!"

Cold wind swirled through the ravine, either funneled naturally or manipulated by Jun's smooth movements up above. The hot, coppery scent of fresh blood filled the air and all three werewolves whirled toward Dominic.

The Bitch snarled at her pack, but even she couldn't contend with the promise of blood. The werewolves charged in a frenzy. Holding his bleeding hand up like a standard, Dominic raced through the interlocking circles of my spell. He was limping from his barely-controlled descent into the ravine, but my assistant stepped carefully and deftly over every charcoal rune.

The cursed wolves chased after Dominic in blind bloodlust. I gauged their speed and carefully calculated my timing. I raised my voice in the final syllables of the incantation, intoning the sounds of the universe in short, controlled bursts. The werewolves crossed over the edge of the circle just as Dominic leapt clear and I completed the spell.

Space twisted in on itself as my magic took hold. Leaves and fragments of crumbling asphalt rose up all around us, floating as though underwater. There was a whoosh of displaced air, a flash of colorless light, and then reality snapped back into place. Everything fell to the ground once more and my spell circle was empty.

But the great black shadow of the Bitch stood just outside the interlocking circles. The rest of her pack was gone, teleported away to the Tower, but the Bitch hadn't followed Dominic's bait into the reach of my spell.

She howled again, that terrible sound of loss that turned my blood to ice in my veins and brought tears to my eyes. Behind me, Dominic swore loudly.

"Stefano!" Jun cried. "Stand clear!"

She raised her hands up in a single swift movement and the walls of the ravine shuddered. Jun had told us that the geomancers summoned spirits to fight werewolves... or buried them alive under the earth.

The Bitch had her back to Jun. Her bright yellow-gold eyes fixed on me and burned with hatred. *I* was the one who had taken her pack away. The huge black and silver monster fell to all fours and lowered her belly to the ground for a pounce. It was all the opening that Jun needed to finish the job. She could finally kill the last were-wolf, bury her here outside Belosnezhka and free the world from the demons' curse.

But Jun's hands shook. She spun in a tight circle, dropped her hands down into a defensive guard and raked her foot across the ground as she called upon the power of the ley lines. The ravine didn't close up around the Bitch. Instead, the sheer end sloped out into a smooth, steep ramp of earth and Jun launched herself down it toward us.

The Bitch leapt at me and Jun's heel connected with her snout mid-air, snapping the werewolf's head to one side. Blood flew from the Bitch's nose. Jun landed and threw a spinning back kick at the monster's stomach, but it was like kicking a brick wall. The Bitch grunted and didn't give a single inch of ground. She lashed out and Jun barely ducked the razor-tipped paw in time.

I snatched for the backup revolver, but Dominic grabbed my shoulder and snatched the gun from my holster. He brandished it as he sprinted past me.

"We can hold her off," he called out. "Just tell us when to get clear of... whatever you're going to do."

Dominic turned toward the Bitch as the big black wolf swatted Jun away and fixed her furious golden gaze on me again. He fired and my gun thundered in his grip. The bullet went wide, barely singing the Bitch's midnight fur. Dominic braced the gun with his bloody hand, winced and fired again.

This time, the shot was good and blasted a red crater into the Bitch's broad chest. She snarled in pain, but the wound was already healing shut. Werewolves were fueled by rage, and the Bitch had plenty of that. Unless Dominic started aiming for her head or heart, all he could do was buy me time.

Which was exactly what Jun and Dominic were doing – buying precious seconds and waiting for me to figure out how to finish this. I wished that I had the time to marvel at their faith.

I jumped back as the geomancer whirled in close, laying into the Bitch with a flurry of punches and kicks too fast to see. Dominic fired a shot into the huge werewolf's shoulder that didn't stop her from leaping at him, claws and fangs bared. Jun swept open hands through the air like fans and a sudden gust of hurricane-force winds drove the Bitch back down to the ground mere feet away from Dominic.

What could I do? Jun and Dominic were good, but they couldn't fight the Bitch for twelve minutes while I prepared another teleportation spell. I could mix a fireball in a minute or two, but the brimstone had been in Dominic's pack. And a fireball wasn't going to stop the Bitch unless she swallowed it. Even then, I wasn't sure.

Desperately, I patted down my pockets, but our supplies were running thin. The only spell I had prepared was the passion charm in my wallet and that was...

Perfect.

Not to cast on myself, but on the Bitch. Now, I know what you're thinking: a horny werewolf is still impassioned. Lust had ignited Dominic's curse once before and I'm not Lilith. I could never survive fucking a werewolf.

But I could alter the passion charm. I could change it. If I inverted the runes – like I did between a seeking spell and an illusion – I would turn the charm inside-out to calm passions instead of enflame them. A werewolf without her passions reverted to human. Altering spells was dangerous, though, and doing it without a lot of testing in a secure sanctum doubly so.

Jun clung to the Bitch, one arm hooked around her tree-trunk neck, and tried to yank her back from Dominic. The great werewolf plucked Jun off like an annoying insect and flung her away. Jun flew through the air and smashed into the ravine wall hard enough to make the whole landscape shiver. She slid to the ground in a shower of rocks and earth. The geomancer struggled to her feet and nearly fell again as she charged at the Bitch.

Dominic was limping and blood ran from the cut across the back of his hand, dripping red into the dirt. He fired a silver shot into the Bitch's knee, but the demon wolf was still moving inexorably forward – toward me and toward all one thousand people of Belosnezhka.

I dug my wallet from my back pants pocket and pulled out the passion charm inside. I unfolded the little square of parchment against the side of the ravine and drew my hunting knife. The parchment of a passion charm was steeped for a full night in the smoke of ginseng and mistletoe... If I damaged it now, the spell would be useless.

My pulse thundered in my ears as I eased the blade over the berkana rune in the center, painstakingly scraping away the sigil there. When I had opened a blank spot in the heart of my spell, I felt along the row of charcoal in my pocket. Not ebony – the hard black wood was full of raw power.

No, changing the passion charm called for something more delicate. I snatched the slender gray stick of burnt rosewood, took a deep breath, and drew the inverted berkana rune into the middle of my new spell.

The Bitch grabbed for Jun with claws like sharpened crescent moons. When the geomancer spun and ducked away, she slammed a huge black knee up into her stomach. Jun hit the ground hard, gasping for breath.

Dominic's gun was empty and clicking hollowly as he pulled the trigger. Swearing, he flung my revolver uselessly at the Bitch and grabbed Jun's arm. Dominic heaved her back upright, but not out of the Bitch's path. They bravely, foolishly held their ground as the last werewolf stalked toward us down the ravine.

Passion charms required physical contact with the target. That was simple when I cast them on myself, but now I had to get close enough to touch a raging lycanthrope.

"Jun!" I shouted. "Bury the Bitch!"

The retreating geomancer very nearly missed her footing and fell again. She staggered and stared at me. Even Dominic risked a potentially lethal look back at me, his eyes wide.

"What?" Jun gasped.

"Just immobilize her," I said. "Trust me!"

Jun dropped to her knees, brought her palms down against the ground, and the earth split open beneath the Bitch. The werewolf fell and Jun's pit slammed shut around her like the jaws of some even larger beast. An earth djinn couldn't have done it better.

I ran toward the Bitch. Jun had buried her to the shoulders, pinning her arms and legs. But the ground buckled and heaved as the huge werewolf wrenched against her prison. Deep cracks already spread out across the road around her, growing wider by the second.

The Bitch howled and screamed in fury. I threw myself down onto one knee before her like a man proposing, but she snapped savagely at me and Dominic fell in beside me to fling an arm across the werewolf's deadly muzzle.

"Get her, boss!" Dominic grunted.

"Hold her still," I said.

"I'm trying...!"

It was like putting a postage stamp on an out-of-control car, but I managed to press the square of parchment into the pitch-black fur of the Bitch's brow. Her burning golden eyes rolled wildly and she fought against the earth like a true demon. Jun's fingers dug into the ground and she groaned with the effort of containing the demon wolf's rage.

"It's going to be okay," I promised. "This is almost over."

I tore the parchment and the winter air filled with the smell of ginseng... But the rich scent that usually made my blood boil was smoother now, like taking a long drink of tea. My spell flowed into the Bitch and she whimpered as all the anger, the hatred and pain that fueled her transformation fell away.

The demonic fire in the Bitch's eyes guttered and died. Fur and claws vanished to be replaced by scarred and dirt-smeared skin. Her body collapsed in on itself, shrinking until the eleven-foot-tall monster was just a middle-aged woman curled up at the bottom of a hole in the road.

"Jun?" I asked. "Are you alright?"

The geomancer rose on unsteady legs and nodded. "I am fine."

"Dominic?"

"Still curse-free, I think," he said, flashing me a thumbs-up and a weary grin. "And I even have all my fingers. That was some sweet magic, boss."

Carefully, I removed my coat and then slid down into the hole. The woman who had been the Bitch lay naked at the bottom, but she was shaking and shivering too hard to be unconscious. I draped my coat around her bare shoulders and she burst into motion, slamming me back into the wall of Jun's pit. She clutched at my throat and tears cut tracks down her dirty cheeks.

"You took my family!" she cried. "You took them away and left me alone...!"

My spells should have quelled her passions. How much pain was this woman in that she could *still* weep and scream for what she had lost? And how long until she transformed again?

"Your family died twelve years ago," I grunted through the dirty fingers closing on my trachea. "I'm sorry, but... but they're gone."

My eyes stung, but it wasn't the pain of her fingernails digging into my skin or the lack of air in my aching lungs. I knew her pain, the loss of my mother and father, of everything I loved. I understood why she fought *never* to feel that pain ever again, how it drove her to embrace the very curse that had killed her family. My vision was going gray around the edges.

"You're not alone," I told her. "And neither am I."

She smashed me back into the wall of the pit, squeezing my throat until I saw stars, but then something cracked against the top of her head with a loud, dull thud. The woman went limp and I wrapped my arms around her to keep her from hitting the ground.

Dominic leaned over the edge of the hole above me. He had retrieved his shotgun and now held it by the barrel, poised to deliver another blow if the first one didn't do the job.

"You tell her, dude," Dominic said.

"I just did," I groaned, rubbing my head. "Jun, can you get us out of here now?"

Chapter
SEVENTEEN

eijing Capital International Airport was a sprawling complex of clean white buildings with arched roofs that managed to make the place feel open and airy despite the massive crowds. The soft burble of artfully placed fountains was completely lost in the chorus of voices, but they looked nice.

A family posed in front of the cascading water, laughing and struggling to hold their positions while one of the kids tried to explain to his parents how to use a selfie stick... which I knew only because Dominic had already explained it to me.

We stood beside a wrought-iron sculpture of four dragons, their claws supporting a sphere engraved in a network of strange lines. The ley lines of Earth, perhaps? Or maybe it was just a piece of art. I looked over Dominic's shoulder and out across the packed airport.

"Jun's walking up behind me, isn't she?" Dominic asked.

I nodded. "How could you tell?"

"You started smiling."

Dominic turned as Jun wove her way through the crowd toward us, a sheaf of papers clutched in one hand. She smiled and gave Dominic a hug, then pulled me down into a short, hard kiss. My head was spinning when Jun released me.

"Thanks for arranging the lift," Dominic said, barely concealing an idiot grin.

We had used the last of our teleportation reagents sending the Bitch to the Tower to be imprisoned and, eventually, cured of her demonic curse. So our journey out of Les Krovi had involved a long ride in the back of a Belosnezhka farmer's truck and a lot of gratitude to the geomancers for helping us get a flight home.

Jun led us across the smooth-polished white floor of the airport toward our gate, handing out plane tickets and pre-stamped customs forms as we walked.

"It is the least we can do," she said. "The last werewolves have finally been captured by the joint efforts of the College and the geomancers. Within the year, their curse will be eradicated."

"No more werewolves," Dominic agreed. He no longer bothered to hide his grin. "We did it! Fuck yeah!"

"So... what now?" Jun asked.

She was looking at me, not Dominic. I drew a deep breath and stopped in front of the gate that matched our tickets.

"There are still vampires in the world. They may not be cursed, but they carry demonic blood. And other monsters, too – yeti, wyverns and dangerous spirits. I'm not out of a job just yet," I said, and then turned to Dominic. "And if *you* still want a job, you had better keep studying."

Dominic's green eyes widened. "Are you saying I can be your apprentice?"

"Let's not go that far," I said.

"Your partner, then?"

"Partners," I agreed.

I raised my fist and held it out to him. Dominic cheered and bumped his knuckles against mine. He earned it.

There was no line for the private flight that the geomancers had chartered for us. No excuse to linger and try to articulate all of the things I longed to say to Jun. All too soon, it was time to leave.

I was going home victorious, my lifelong quest finally fulfilled. I was happy – beyond happy – but something inside me still ached hollowly.

"We have taken care of everything on this end," Jun said. She held up one stack of customs papers. "Will there be any trouble with the weapons or reagents when landing in America?"

"No," I told her, shaking my head. "I've contacted the College and they've made all the usual arrangements."

"Then my swords will not be a problem?" Jun asked.

"Your... swords?"

I repeated the words while my brain churned, trying to make sense of Jun's question. I had missed something. Something important, to judge by the way Dominic's hands flew to his mouth.

"I was hoping you wouldn't mind another partner," Jun said.

Her cheeks were bright red and her lower lip trembled just a little, like she was afraid I might say no.

"But... Jun, are you sure?" I stammered. "You said that returning to your training, earning your tattoos... that was what you wanted when you got away from Ptah's palace."

"I did," said Jun. "And I used those skills to help rid the world of werewolves. But there is something else that I want, Stefano. I want you."

I dropped my bag and papers to grab Jun in both arms, lifting her up into the air. She wound her legs around my waist and kissed me. I met her kiss with everything I had left inside me. Love isn't something that even our magic can measure or define, but Jun understood every word I might never know how to say.

Dominic cheered and pointed at us. He jumped up and down, announcing our new partnership to the entire airport. I kissed Jun until neither of us could breathe anymore and didn't let go until my phone rang for the second time.

Finally, I set Jun back down onto the ground, but held her close while I fished the cell phone out of my pocket. Dominic must have charged it for me. I swiped the green button and both Dominic and Jun leaned in to listen.

"Stefano," said Dorian Vandi. "We need you back at the College immediately."

"We're about to board the plane now," I told the High Magus. "What is it? Did Lilith find another werewolf? One that we missed?"

"No. We're calling everyone back, every wizard of the College and the Castle."

"Why?" I asked. "What happened?"

"Arthur Pendragon is missing from Avalon."

For more stories by
Natalie and Eric Severine,
visit us at **LLStories.com**

www.ingramcontent.com/pod-product-compliance
Lightning Source LLC
Chambersburg PA
CBHW030631120726
47904CB00006B/2112